***Tim swaggered over to Kari.
"Is he the reason
you dumped me?"***

"One has nothing to do with the other."

"Oh, really?" Tim smirked and his eyes narrowed nastily. "You're so hung up on that dumb cowboy, you can't think straight."

Kari was infuriated to hear John referred to as a dumb cowboy. "I'm not hung up on him," she said. "He is just someone I work with at the clinic. And another thing, he is not a dumb cowboy. He is studying to be an equine veterinarian."

"That's just perfect." Tim started laughing. "You can mess up the horses, and he can stitch them back together."

Kari had never hit anyone in her whole life, but her fingers itched to slap Tim....

Caprice Romances from Tempo Books

A CAPRICE ROMANCE

Just Like a Dream
Eileen Stacy

TEMPO BOOKS, NEW YORK

JUST LIKE A DREAM

A Tempo Book/published by arrangement with
the author

PRINTING HISTORY
Tempo Original/June 1985

ISBN: 0-441-49549-4

"Caprice" and the stylized Caprice logo are trademarks
belonging to The Berkley Publishing Group.

Tempo Books are published by The Berkley Publishing Group,
200 Madison Avenue, New York, New York 10016.
Tempo Books are registered in the United States Patent Office.
PRINTED IN THE UNITED STATES OF AMERICA

1

KARI STEWART tried to imagine herself in a large show ring as she trotted her Quarter horse, Poco, around the small enclosure. Her jeans and flannel shirt became a fancy brocade riding suit and the hill rising away from the paddock was a grandstand. The fence posts were spectators lining the rail and marveling at the easy grace of horse and rider. Kari urged Poco into a slow lope. She tilted her head back and enjoyed the gentle May breeze as it brushed her face and lifted her shoulder-length auburn hair.

At a command from the announcer, she reined Poco to a halt and walked the big red gelding to the center of the ring. She lined him up squarely and leaned forward in the saddle to pat his muscular neck. When her number was called, she walked Poco forward to accept her first-place ribbon. As Kari thanked the presenter and reached down for the trophy, a voice called from behind her.

"Are you almost finished?"

Kari started, embarrassed to be caught in the middle of one of her fantasies. If she had to be discovered, why did it have to be by Tim? He already thought she was too much of a dreamer and told her so often.

She turned to wave at the tall, slim boy. He folded his arms along the top rail of the fence and smiled indulgently. Kari turned Poco and trotted him to the fence.

Kari smiled down at Tim. "I wasn't expecting to see you tonight."

Tim motioned in the direction of the driveway. "I just got my car running and took it out for a trial run. I turned her loose and look where we ended up." Tim spread his arms wide and flashed one of his charming smiles.

Kari's green eyes sparkled as she looked down at his smiling face. Tim wasn't what you could really call handsome, not in the classical sense anyway, but when he turned on his charm, Kari couldn't help but think he was good-looking. He had brown hair and hazel eyes, stood nearly six feet tall and was rather thin. His thin body was the perfect build for playing golf, he had once told Kari. Which was exactly what he planned to do all summer—that and drive around in his car.

Tim had a serious side, too, although Kari rarely saw it. She knew he planned to be an engineer like her father. Often since they had started dating, Tim had brought over his trigonometry homework to get her father's help.

Kari dismounted and pulled the reins over Poco's head. As she started toward the barn, Tim fell into step beside her. Even in her riding boots, the top of Kari's head came to just above his shoulder and she had to tilt her head back to look him in the face.

"So what was wrong with the car?" she asked.

Tim's face lit up. "I've been rebuilding the carburetor." He loved talking about his car, and given the opportunity, he launched into a detailed account of exactly what he had done.

Kari knew very little about cars and let her mind wander as he talked. She liked Tim. They'd been dating for several months, and it seemed to Kari that having Tim for a boyfriend had changed her life for the better. In a small high school like Brookview, having a boyfriend as well-liked as Tim automatically made you important, too. Where she had received very few invitations before, Kari now found herself invited to all sorts of parties. Of course, she couldn't accept all the invitations—her parents were very strict about her dating on school nights.

Tim stopped when they reached the small barn, wrinkling his nose in displeasure. "I think I'll wait for you out here."

Kari tugged at his arm. "Oh, come on, city slicker. I just cleaned the stalls last night. The only things you're going to smell are leather and clean horses."

Tim followed Kari reluctantly into the barn. He leaned his lanky frame against one of the support posts and watched as Kari tied Poco in a cross-tie. She uncinched the girth and pulled the heavy Western saddle from the horse's back.

Tim sprang forward. "Here, let me help you with that."

He grabbed the saddle and looked at Kari questioningly. "Now that I have it, what do I do with it?"

Kari laughed and pointed in the direction of a small room.

"It goes in there. That's the tack room."

Tim disappeared into the small room, only to reappear a moment later waving a handful of papers. "What's all this?"

Kari peered over Poco's back at Tim's waving hand. "Show bills," she answered. "I've been collecting as many as I can for all the shows coming up in the next couple of months."

"Shows—you mean like in the horse shows?" Tim looked puzzled. "You mean you're actually going to show that horse?"

Kari stopped brushing Poco's sleek red hide. "And just what is wrong with this horse?"

"Nothing, I guess. It's just that—well, you haven't done very much of that kind of thing, have you?"

"Not until now." Kari picked up the soft face brush and moved to Poco's head. "But now that I have Poco, all that is going to change."

Tim walked around Poco, being careful to leave a clear distance between himself and the horse's hindquarters. "I thought you said he was a little rough in the ring."

Kari nodded her agreement. "He's a little funny about his head, but I'll work that out of him."

"And where does that leave me?" Tim demanded. "What am I supposed to do while you're working that out of him and running off to these silly horse shows every weekend?"

"They're not silly and besides it won't be every weekend. We're not that good, and I couldn't afford it anyway."

Tim didn't look convinced. Kari took the show bills from his hand and leafed through them.

"Look!" Kari fanned the bills out for him to see. "Most of them are for Sunday afternoons. That leaves me free in the evenings and almost every Saturday."

"Sunday afternoons are the couples' golf tournaments at the club. I sort of hoped you would play as my partner."

Kari sighed and folded up the show bills. "Tim, my parents can't afford to join that country club, and even if we did belong, I don't play golf well enough to enter a tournament."

"I can take you as my guest. If I give you pointers, you can improve your game in no time. I mean, look, we could practice every afternoon as soon as school is out."

Kari looked at him helplessly. "I can't play golf every day. I'm going to have to work this summer."

"Work? Oh, yeah, to pay for the horse shows, right?" Tim stalked across the barn and sat down on a bale of straw.

Kari followed him. "That's part of it, yes. But mostly it's for college. My parents said they could handle my board and tuition, but I would have to pay for my books and other supplies. And if I wanted any new clothes, I'd have to buy them."

"You have a whole year before you'll be going to college," Tim protested.

"Right, and that's only two summers to work. So I'd better start saving now. I have a lot of school ahead of me if I plan to be a vet."

Tim looked stricken. "A vet, like in veterinarian? You can't be serious." He chuckled and Kari was hurt by the sarcastic edge to his laugh.

"And why not?" she demanded, her jaw set in a stubborn line.

"Because girls don't become veterinarians. At least not with horses, they don't."

Kari's eyes narrowed as she viewed a facet of Tim she had not previously noticed. Her patience growing thin, she returned to her horse and continued to brush the sleek hide. She knew it was hopeless to try to reason with him. She slipped the bridle from Poco's head and turned him into the stall. Poco lowered his head and thumped it against the hard-rubber feeding tub in the corner.

"Be patient," Kari scolded as she scooped a measure of grain from the bin and dumped it into the feed bucket.

Kari turned to Tim. "All finished."

Tim jumped down from the bale of straw and followed her from the barn. They walked several steps before he grabbed her hand, pulling her to a halt. As she turned to face him, he smiled sheepishly. Then he placed one hand on each of her shoulders and gazed at her intently. "It's just that you spend so much time with that silly animal, maybe I'm a little jealous."

Kari stared at him for a long moment, then her lips relaxed into a smile. "You shouldn't be, though," she teased. "I'm not the least bit jealous of your golf clubs."

Tim laughed and everything seemed back to normal. Bending his head, he kissed her lightly. Kari leaned toward him and raised her face to his. This time his kiss lingered, warm and gentle on her lips, and Kari felt comfort in the knowledge that Tim was her boyfriend.

Tim pulled back quickly when a voice hailed them from the edge of the pasture. Kari wobbled a little when he drew away.

She regained her balance and stole a quick glance up at him, but he wasn't looking in her direction. He was busy watching her friend, Lynn Williams, as she walked across the pasture. Her long, silky blond hair caught the sunlight as she tossed it over her shoulder. Lynn looked great in her tight-fitting designer jeans and pale-blue turtleneck sweater. Kari suddenly felt very sloppy and shapeless in her work jeans and flannel shirt. She couldn't help but notice Tim's admiring glance as Lynn stopped in front of him.

Kari searched for something to say. "What time are we leaving for the meeting?"

Now she had Tim's full attention again. But as he turned, his smile faded. "What meeting? I thought you were going to test-drive my car with me. Then I thought maybe we could study together. There are a couple of things I need to ask your father about."

"I can't tonight, Tim. I have the Ohio Junior Riders' meeting. I told you about it last week."

Tim threw his hands in the air. "Horses. Every time I see you, you have to do something with horses. I thought girls outgrew horses when they turned twelve or thirteen. . . . You're nearly seventeen, Kari. Don't you think it's time to grow up a little?" Tim turned on his heel and strode away.

Kari could feel the hot tears burning the back of her eyelids. She sniffed and blinked them back. Was she being childish? She wasn't sure. But she did know that there were lots of girls on the circuit older than her, and they didn't seem the least bit childish.

Kari sighed and her shoulders drooped. Lynn draped an arm around her. "Don't mind him, he'll be back. Besides, he should have called first."

Kari looked at her friend. Lynn was right. Tim should have called first, but he rarely did. He just showed up and expected her to be at his beck and call.

"I'm afraid he does that all the time," explained Kari. "I've thought about saying something, but I didn't want to make him angry."

Lynn shook her head vehemently and stared hard at her. "No, it wouldn't pay to make him too angry. Tim is really popular around school, and he is your first real boyfriend. Besides, I think he's really cute, and no one is perfect."

Kari knew popularity was important to Lynn, although she

rarely stated it so bluntly. She watched her friend's reaction as she explained, "I'm not interested in Tim's popularity." Even as she said it, Kari knew the statement wasn't entirely true. She felt important being seen with Tim. "He's fun to be with," she continued. "At least most of the time." Kari shrugged her shoulders helplessly. "It's that we have a problem with hobbies. He doesn't want to have a thing to do with what I'm interested in, but he thinks I should share all his interests."

"His interests, like going to the country club?"

Kari nodded.

Lynn flipped her long hair over her shoulder. "Well, if you want my opinion, I think you should go to the club with him every chance you get. A lot of really cute boys go there." She paused thoughtfully. "You're really lucky to have Tim for a boyfriend. He could help you get places. I'd be careful not to blow it."

Kari and Lynn walked across the backyard to the house. Kari only half listened to Lynn's chatter about her latest boyfriend as she thought about Tim. Maybe if she had dated more she would have known how to handle the situation better. Lynn didn't have that problem. It seemed to Kari that she was never lacking for dates. A different boy was chasing her every week. Kari envied her friend's popularity with the opposite sex. Maybe Lynn was right about Tim. After all, she did have a lot more experience with boys than Kari.

Tim had never really pursued Kari; they just sort of drifted together. They met at school the day before Christmas break at a dance sponsored by the school. From experience, the teachers knew nothing would be learned those last few hours before classes ended. All the teachers except Miss Mender, that is. Her morning French and English classes went on as usual. No one was listening, of course, except for maybe Anita Hart, super brain of the junior class.

Kari remembered sitting in French class that morning watching the seniors goof off every time Miss Mender turned her back to conjugate a verb on the blackboard.

Tim was one of eight seniors in the class picking up his last language requirement for college entrance. He hadn't seemed to notice Kari before that morning. She was sitting in the same seat she always took—last seat, last row, right by the door. She had Phys Ed the period before, so she usually arrived at class just as the bell rang and slipped quietly into her seat.

She knew who Tim was, though—everyone in school knew him. He was one of the most popular boys in the senior class, but that knowledge had not impressed Kari before. She had very little interest in boys and was still waiting to experience that glorious feeling her friends called love.

Maybe that's why Tim had never noticed her before—not Tim or any other boy for that matter. Boys tended to steer clear of girls who constantly had their noses buried in horse books, especially medical horse books. Until Tim came along, Kari could count the dates she had had on one hand.

But that changed the day in December when Tim turned in his seat to make several comments to his friends. Kari figured she must have been in his line of vision. He glanced directly at her several times and then looked her straight in the eyes and smiled—that wonderful smile that won over every girl who came under its radiant charm. Kari felt a silly confusion as she smiled back. A popular boy had never looked at her that way before. The heat of a blush spread up her neck and turned her ruddy cheeks a bright red. She was relieved when Miss Mender finished writing on the blackboard and Tim was forced to turn and face the front of the room.

That afternoon, when Kari walked into the multipurpose room where the dance was being held, she spotted Tim immediately. He was on the far side of the room talking to a group of seniors. Tim was usually surrounded by a large group of friends. He had a way of charming everyone when it was to his advantage. Kari remembered he had glanced in her direction, but hadn't really acknowledged her presence. So she was totally surprised when he approached her a few minutes later and asked her to dance. They spent the rest of the afternoon dancing and talking, and suddenly, they were a twosome. Kari tried to think back to exactly how it had happened. The afternoon had gone by so fast that it was a pleasant blur of confusion.

Kari was brought back to the present by Lynn's laugh.

"Have you heard a thing I've been saying?" she scolded. "You looked as though you were a million miles away."

"Of course, I was listening," Kari lied.

The girls had reached the back porch. Lynn waved goodbye and started across the backyard to her own house next door.

"I'll pick you up in an hour," Lynn called back as she reached her house.

Kari let the back door slam shut behind her and trudged up the steps to her room.

"Kari, is that you?" her mother called from the kitchen. "Hurry and change so you'll have time to eat something before you leave."

Kari quickly shed her riding clothes and climbed into the shower. She let the warm water spray over her shoulders as she closed her eyes. The pulsating spray began to relax her, and she realized the argument with Tim had upset her more than she first thought.

As Kari was toweling herself dry, her younger sister stuck her head around the door. "Mind if I come in?"

Kari motioned her in, and Pam took up a seat on the clothes hamper. "Are you going to the meeting tonight?" she asked.

Kari nodded. "Do you want to come?" She slipped into her pink shorty bathrobe and headed down the hall to her bedroom.

Pam followed. "You bet. There are some pretty terrific guys in that club." She smiled devilishly as she plopped down on Kari's white ruffled bedspread. Pam was three years younger and was just beginning to realize boys could be fun to have around sometimes, a fact Kari had been slow to admit.

Kari quickly tugged on her best pair of jeans. She pulled a mint-green sweater from her drawer and slipped it over her head. Green was her best color, or so everyone told her. They said it made her green eyes look greener.

Kari examined herself in her full-length door mirror and made a face. She didn't have a bad figure, a little on the slim side maybe, but she sure didn't fill out a sweater the way Lynn did.

Pam giggled as she watched her sister. "You could always stuff tissues down your sweater."

Kari picked up a lavender pillow and tossed it playfully at her sister. The pillow hit Pam in the head. She quickly retaliated, starting a pillow fight.

Their mother interrupted their silliness as she called from the kitchen, "Are you girls almost ready? I'm putting dinner on the table."

"Almost ready," both girls answered in unison.

Kari sighed and walked back to her dresser. She picked up a brush and ran it through her curly, coppery hair. It was one of her better features, she had to admit. She feathered back the sides and sprayed on a dab of hair spray to hold them in place.

She picked up her peach lip gloss and examined herself once more in the mirror. Not perfect, but not too bad either.

Kari grabbed her purse, and she and Pam ran down the stairs.

Mr. Stewart walked in the back door as the girls reached the bottom of the steps. He hung his sports coat and tie on the closet doorknob and went to the kitchen to find Mrs. Stewart, while Kari and Pam exchanged knowing smiles. It had been the same for as long as they could remember. When their father arrived home in the evening, he went straight to the kitchen to give their mother a big bear hug and a kiss. Now that was real love, Kari thought, as she watched her mother and father. After all the years they had been married, they still seemed so much in love. Kari wondered if she would ever find love like that. Oh, she had Tim, and she cared for him, a lot, but she didn't think she loved him.

Kari and her sister sat down at the table and hurriedly filled their plates.

Their father eyed them critically as they quickly shoveled the food into their mouths. "You girls going somewhere?"

"Junior Riders' meeting," Pam managed between bites.

"Oh, the horse club." Mr. Stewart nodded his approval. "Sarah, you were right when you said that as long as we kept them interested in horses, we wouldn't have to worry about boys." He winked at their mother.

"Now, Dave, boys belong to the horse club, too." Mrs. Stewart reached over and patted her husband's hand. "I just believe riding is an active, healthy sport."

"Healthy for whom?" Kari's father asked. His fork paused above his plate. "Let's see. Since the girls have had their horses, you've gotten a black eye from Pam's pony, a broken foot from the old mare and a sprained wrist from Kari's gelding. I think that about covers the healthy activities." He smiled at Kari. "Those horses can cause more trouble than the jet planes I help design."

Kari watched the friendly teasing between her parents as she finished dinner.

Both her parents had been very understanding about the horses. When they moved to the five-acre tract outside the small town of Brookview, they promised Kari and Pam a horse. In less than a year an old buckskin mare moved into the back-yard. A year later, the old mare was followed by a chubby

Welsh pony for Pam. Then Kari and her sister joined the 4-H
Club and started showing their horses at neighborhood shows.
After they gained some experience, they decided to get a couple
of registered Quarter horses to take to the larger shows.

Only a year had passed since Pam had emptied her savings
account to buy a weanling Quarter mare. She wouldn't be able
to ride her for another year, but the mare already showed
promise.

About the same time, Kari sold her gentle old mare to the
family who owned the tract on the other side of Lynn's family.
They had two small children who spoiled the old horse, and
Kari knew she had a good home. It was like not really selling
Lady Buck at all, since Kari saw her almost every day. She
took the money from the sale along with some she had saved
from baby-sitting and bought Poco.

Kari would never forget the afternoon the farm delivered
the sorrel Quarter horse. She had felt so proud leading the
prancing gelding across the back lawn to show Lynn.

It had been four years since the first horse had stepped onto
the Stewart property, and as Kari's father often said, "Life has
never been quite the same."

A car horn sounded from the driveway.

"That must be Lynn," Kari said. She jumped up and carried
her plate to the sink. "See you all later." She grabbed her purse
and ran out the back door. Pam followed close behind.

2

LYNN WAS bursting with excitement when Kari and Pam climbed into the Williams' subcompact. "I've got the greatest news. I've found a summer job. Or I should say, my father found one for me."

Kari fastened her seatbelt and gave Lynn her full attention.

"Oh, wait until you hear! It's just going to be the best summer yet." Lynn's face was animated with excitement. "The country club has hired my dad to manage the pool and concessions for the summer. And he hired me to run the snack bar. What do you think?"

Kari forced a smile. "That's great." She was happy for her friend, but a little depressed for herself. She had put in job applications all over town and hadn't heard anything. With the university so close by, most of the summer jobs went to the college students.

"Do you think he might have a position for me?" Kari ventured.

"I already asked," Lynn said seriously. "Dad says the kids who belong to the country club get first crack at the jobs. He already has a stack of applications on his desk, although I can't imagine some of those kids working."

Kari thought she detected a note of bitterness in Lynn's voice. Her father had a good job as the basketball coach and boys' Phys Ed teacher at Brookview High, but several times Kari had gotten the impression that Lynn wished her father had a better-paying job. Kari didn't think it was all that important, but then she had never been very concerned about appearances for appearances' sake. Being popular was very important to Lynn, and Kari knew there were times when her best friend spent too much money on clothes. Kari thought it was a little silly, but everyone had their own dreams. Many times her

friends looked at her strangely when she mentioned she wanted
to be a vet.

Kari looked over at her friend, and Lynn's face was all
smiles again. "Just think, working around all those gorgeous
popular guys who belong to the club. And being around the
pool all summer, I'm bound to get a fantastic tan."

Kari could visualize Lynn lounging around the pool with
her beautiful tan, basking in the attention from all the single
guys. It was the perfect job for her friend. Kari drifted off into
a daydream. Instead of Lynn sitting in the deck chair, it was
Kari. She was wearing an emerald-green bikini which accen-
tuated her red hair and green eyes. Her hair was piled on top
of her head and she wore designer sunglasses. As she pulled
a bottle of suntan lotion from her beach bag, several boys
offered to rub it on her back. She dismissed them with a bored
motion of her hand. Two more boys showed up carrying cold
drinks and Kari selected an iced lemonade.

A faint smile crossed Kari's lips at the fantasy she had
conjured up. Being chased by one boy would be exciting, but
to be pursued by several would be more than Kari could handle.
She had always felt a little insecure around boys and never
liked being the center of attention. Besides, sitting around the
pool all day would get boring. She would rather be doing
something with the horses.

The crunch of gravel beneath the tires signaled Kari that
they had reached their destination. Lynn drove over a cattle
guard and under a sign identifying the Pinemeadows Quarter
Horse Farm. She braked to a stop by a small building where
several cars were already parked.

"Looks like there's going to be a good turnout tonight,"
Lynn said.

Kari nodded as she got out and slammed the car door. She
surveyed the large group of people gathered around the work
ring. Several people waved and Kari waved back. "Looks like
there's going to be an interesting demonstration topic tonight."

Lynn laughed. "Oh, that's not it; I guarantee you." She
made a face. "We're going to learn all about hoof care."

"Yuck!" Kari wrinkled her nose. "I already know enough
about hoof care to write my own book. What else can they tell
me?"

"I doubt if it's for us old-timers." Pam struck a decrepit,
bent-over pose. "It's probably for the new kids on the block."

Lynn and Kari both laughed. Pam had only been a member herself for a few months.

"Well, we could always duck out early," suggested Lynn. She smoothed her hair and headed in the direction of the work ring.

"No dice." Kari pointed to the ring. Their advisor had just led a sleek bay mare into the wood-slatted enclosure. "I think Mr. Cooper is on to us. Looks like he has the demo planned first."

The girls reached the ring. Kari rested her elbows on the top rail and groaned. "Everything you ever wanted to know about hoof care, but were afraid to ask."

The girls laughed, and several club members joined in the joking. They all took seats on one side of the ring. Some perched on the top rail of the fence while others sat on the ground. Kari chose a spot where a few bales of straw were stacked. Lynn and Pam joined her.

A blond boy, a little younger than Kari, sprawled on the bale of straw in front of her. "Hey, Kari, how's the big red beast doing?"

Kari wrinkled her nose. "He's coming along fine, Steve. He doesn't always want to keep his head down, but we're working on it."

"So, turn him into a barrel racer. With the speed that horse has, he'd be a sure winner."

Kari shook her head. "I want to show Western Pleasure and Horsemanship."

"Such a waste!" Steve clutched his chest and fell back dramatically. Then he turned his attention to Pam. "Maybe you can convince her of the error of her ways."

Kari looked at her sister and noticed the pink flush on her cheeks as she fumbled for something to say. Now Kari knew who Pam meant when she said the club had some cute boys.

She came to her sister's rescue as she asked, "What's wrong with showing Western Pleasure and Horsemanship?"

Steve's eyes widened in mock surprise. "I'll tell you what's wrong. No excitement. The contest events are where it's at— barrel racing, pole bending . . . You could still show him in Horsemanship if you wanted. The judge will be grading only you, but Western Pleasure . . . that's another story. The horse's performance is everything, and if he even sours an ear, you lose points. I'll take contest any day."

Kari shrugged and turned her attention back to Mr. Cooper. He had taken out a clipboard and was casually taking an attendance check when she received a sharp jab in the ribs from Lynn's elbow.

"Who's that?" Lynn whispered.

Kari glanced in the direction of Lynn's stare. Her eyes focused on one of the handsomest boys she had ever seen in her life. He walked up to the ring and ducked between two of the wooden slats. Kari guessed he was about Tim's height, but his shoulders were broader and his build more muscular. His hair was dark, almost black, and fell carelessly across his forehead. It was a sharp contrast to the bright-red Western shirt he wore under his denim jacket. He leaned against one of the fence posts and hooked his thumbs in the front pockets of his Levi's.

Steve's gaze followed the direction of the girls' stare. "Oh, that's our new junior advisor."

"Junior advisor?" questioned Lynn. "I didn't know we had one."

"We do now."

Mr. Cooper laid down the clipboard and walked back to the center of the ring. He raised his hands high over his head to get the group's attention.

"Listen up, everyone." He clapped his hands a couple of times and waited for everyone to quiet down. "Okay, Junior Riders, we've got a lot to get done tonight. First, we have a short demonstration for you, then we'll go inside for the meeting. We've got a lot of material to cover for the club's show."

The dark-haired boy pushed himself away from the fence post and walked to the center of the ring. He walked with a strong purposeful stride, his cowboy boots kicking up little wisps of dust as he walked.

Mr. Cooper turned to the boy and put his arm around his shoulders. "And now, I want to introduce our newest member. This is John Garrett." Mr. Cooper patted the boy's shoulder affectionately. "He's going to be sort of a junior advisor for the club."

Kari knew she was staring, but couldn't force herself to look away. It was as though she were caught in a trance. She tried to concentrate on what Mr. Cooper was saying.

"He has been working in a veterinary clinic for the last two years and will be studying pre-veterinary medicine at the university starting in the fall."

Kari's attention was captured immediately. She wondered which university he was going to attend. There were several in the Dayton area, but she thought only one offered veterinary medicine. It was Wittenburg University, the one Kari hoped to go to herself.

Mr. Cooper continued to talk and Kari continued to stare. John glanced in her direction and their eyes met for a brief electrifying second. Were his eyes brown or blue? Kari couldn't be sure. He had caught her staring and she had looked quickly away. Suddenly she felt very flustered and confused.

"John has been showing horses for a number of years," Mr. Cooper went on, "so I think he might be of some help to us."

Mr. Cooper slapped the boy lightly on the back. "Well, John, I'm going to turn this demonstration over to you."

Kari watched as John stepped forward and picked up the horse's lead shank. He twirled the end around his hand as he looked over the group. He had an air of authority and the appearance of one who demanded instant attention.

"Well, I'm sure the word has gotten out," he said in a deep resonant voice. "This demo is going to be on hoof and leg care." The corners of his mouth turned up as if always on the edge of laughter. "I'm sure the way you all feel about this subject was aptly stated by one member when she was overheard to say, "Yuck." John looked pointedly at Kari and smiled broadly.

Kari felt her face turn crimson as a few giggles rippled through the group. She wished she didn't blush so easily.

"And since I'm sure you all feel the same way," John continued, "we're all going to say a big *yuck!* All together now, let's hear it."

Kari's word came back to haunt her. It echoed off the surrounding buildings as the entire club yelled. All except Kari, that is, who hunched lower on her seat and tried to hide behind Steve's cowboy hat.

John laughed. It was a warm, friendly sound that made Kari forget her embarrassment. She glanced up to find John's engaging smile directed at her. His smile was infectious and Kari smiled back. She felt a funny little quiver inside her, and somehow she knew her life had taken on a new dimension.

"Now that we have that out of the way, I'm going to tell you this is not really a demo about hoof care." John led the bay mare closer to the fence and squared her up. "We're going to discuss what occurs when you forget about proper care or when something unforeseen happens."

John turned to face the horse. Kari studied his profile as he turned. His dark hair was swept to one side and fell over his strong forehead. He had a straight nose and a good, strong chin. In fact, he looked just right all over.

Kari watched the easy grace of his body as he moved around the horse. She listened with fascination as he pointed to various parts of the horse's leg and explained their common ailments.

Kari glanced around the semicircle of club members. All their faces were serious, their attention captured by John's knowledge and expert presentation. Kari could tell from the books she had studied that he knew his subject well. But there was something else that attracted her, something intangible, an invisible force that bridged the space between them and touched her with an intensity that made her quiver.

John leaned down and pointed to a section of the mare's hind leg. "Edema results from swelling and a reduction in the blood supply," he was saying.

Steve's hand went up. "So what can you do to keep this from happening?"

John turned in Kari's direction. He glanced at her briefly and a thrill shot through her. Then he answered Steve.

"If your horse takes a bad fall, keep him moving. Don't tie him up and don't put him in a stall right away. If you can't exercise him, at least turn him out in a pasture."

John answered several more questions, then he paused, hands on hips, and waited. "Any more questions?" No one else raised a hand. He smiled, his eyes crinkling at the corners as he did so.

"Okay, then, everyone to the Coke machine."

The crowd dispersed. Most of the kids headed to the small building by the ring. It was where they held their meetings and where Mr. Cooper had installed the old chest-style Coke cooler. He had removed the coin mechanism and kept it stocked with a variety of sodas for the club.

Kari lagged behind to see if John was going to come to the meeting. She busied herself with a make-believe spot on her jeans. Her head was down, and she studied John through her lowered lashes. He stood just a few feet from where she was sitting. As he talked to one of the older boys in the club, she listened to the melodic pitch of his deep voice.

Kari watched as they headed in the direction of the barns. Neither boy seemed to notice her slight figure sitting on the straw. She watched until they were out of sight around the corner of the small club building. Then she ran to catch up with Lynn and Pam.

Kari entered the building and looked around until she spotted Lynn who was leaning against the far wall drinking a Coke. The dark wood paneling made an attractive frame for her blond hair. Several boys stood in a half circle around her.

"She's like a queen bee," muttered Kari, and felt guilty the moment she said it. After all, Lynn was her best friend. It wasn't her fault that boys found her attractive.

Kari found Pam by the Coke machine trying to decide between a diet soda and an Orange Crush. Pam tended to be slightly chubby and had to watch her weight carefully.

"Live it up," said Kari, then reached in and handed her sister the Orange Crush.

"Oh, there you are. I wondered what happened to you."

Kari grabbed a Coke and headed for a chair.

Pam sat down beside her. "What do you think of the new junior advisor? Isn't he a dream?"

"He's all right." Kari tried to force her voice to sound normal, but it came out thin and high-pitched.

Pam eyed her suspiciously. "I think he's got your number. He sure singled you out in a hurry."

Kari felt an incredible excitement. It wasn't just her imagination; he had noticed her. Kari tried to sound casual. "I think he was just trying to loosen everyone up."

Mr. Cooper walked to the front of the room and signaled the group to take their seats.

Pam leaned over and whispered to Kari. "I hope the meeting doesn't last too long. I still have Ohio history homework to do.

Kari frowned at her sister and searched the room for John. His dark head wasn't visible among the other boys, and Kari felt a pang of disappointment.

Just then, the meeting was called to order by the club president, a short pudgy girl with long brown hair. She spoke in a monotone and Kari found her mind wandering. Glancing around the room, she saw silver trophies on wooden shelves and ribbons in every color of the rainbow on the walls. Pictures of the Pinemeadows champions were grouped with silver trays and engraved plaques.

Mr. Cooper had said John showed horses. Kari imagined his walls covered with blue ribbons. She could imagine him sitting straight and tall in the saddle, his horse performing flawlessly as John put him through his paces. And then Kari saw herself beside him on her big sorrel gelding. Poco behaved beautifully. He set his head right and picked up both of his leads. The two horses worked as one as they cantered around the ring. Kari smiled to herself just thinking of it.

The door of the small building squeaked shut, and Kari looked up. John half leaned, half sat on a small table in the corner of the room. He stretched his long legs out in front of him, crossing one boot over the other.

"Come on, you guys," the president was pleading, "won't someone take charge of the awards?" She looked around the room. "I know it's a big job, but . . . Charlie? Bill?"

The boys shook their heads.

Almost without realizing it, Kari timidly raised her hand.

The pudgy girl frowned. "Yes, Kari?"

"I'll do it." Was that her voice? It sounded breathy and uncertain.

"You'll what?" The girl looked surprised.

Kari swallowed and spoke up. "I said, I'll handle the awards."

She saw John look in her direction. He raised his eyebrows in surprise, and then a smile tugged at the corners of his mouth.

Well, I got his attention, thought Kari, but what have I gotten myself into?

The girl at the front of the room was relieved. "That's great," she sighed. "Thanks, Kari. Well, that takes care of all of the committees. Any other business?" Getting no response she banged the gavel. "Meeting adjourned."

Kari sat motionless for several minutes as the realization of what she had volunteered for struck her.

Mr. Cooper sat down beside her. A brief moment of panic gripped her as he laid a heavy packet in her lap.

"All the brochures and order forms are in here," he said, tapping the brown envelope with a stubby finger. "I believe there's also a record of what was ordered last year."

Kari swallowed hard and managed a slight grin. She hoped she wouldn't let Mr. Cooper down.

Gingerly she opened the packet and peered inside.

"You've taken on quite a job." The deep male voice sounded just above her ear as John bent over her shoulder to examine the packet.

Kari's normally steady fingers trembled at the proximity of the handsome boy who leaned close to her. Not trusting her voice, she simply nodded.

John edged between the rows of chairs and lowered his tall frame into the seat next to her. Kari could feel his gaze, but couldn't meet his eyes.

"I hope you can get a couple of the other members to help you," he said. "That's an awful lot for one person to handle."

"Mmm," Kari mumbled. She felt silly and tongue-tied under his close scrutiny.

"Haven't I seen you around the circuit?"

Kari nervously fiddled with the clasp on the envelope as his eyes wandered over her fair skin and auburn hair. "I'm sure two girls couldn't have hair that color."

The aura of self-confidence which emanated from him made Kari feel insecure. She met his eyes briefly.

"Yes, I show a Quarter horse," she answered after some hesitation.

"I thought I'd seen you. You show a stocky sorrel, right?"

John continued to stare, but his mouth relaxed into a mischievous grin. "I hope you didn't mind me picking on you earlier. Sometimes I get carried away. It's one of my character flaws."

Kari realized she had been holding her breath as her face relaxed into a smile. As far as she could see at that moment, he had no flaws.

"What did you say your name is?" he said, continuing to smile at her.

Kari felt again the overpowering magnetism of his closeness. "I didn't say, but it's Kari Stewart."

"Hi, Kari. I was afraid I was just going to have to call you Red." John extended a strong hand to grasp Kari's small one. His touch was gentle, and Kari felt an unbelievable thrill from the brief encounter.

John uncoiled his muscular body from the chair and inclined his head toward the door. "Looks like your friends are waiting.

If you need any help with the awards, let me know."

Kari hugged the envelope to her chest and edged between the row of chairs and John's imposing frame. Carefully, so as not to brush the solid wall of his body with her own, she moved past him, and hurried to meet Lynn and Pam.

3

KARI WOKE earlier than usual the next morning. She had set her alarm extra early to make sure she had enough time to wash and blow-dry her hair before school. Wanting to look her best today, she rummaged through her closet, critically dismissing one outfit after another. It had to be something special, something a little nicer than jeans. After examining her small selection of skirts, she finally selected a pleated, muted-brown plaid. She laid it across her bed along with a chocolate-brown silky blouse. Kari studied her choice. It might be overdoing it a little for school, she thought as she headed to the bathroom, but she had a good reason.

Kari stuck her head under the shower spray and let the warm water drench her scalp. Her thoughts wandered to the coming day. She was sure Tim would be over his anger by this morning, but just in case he was still pouting, she wanted to look special enough to change his mind.

Kari towel-dried the extra moisture from her hair and plugged in her blow dryer.

Pam stumbled into the bathroom. She yawned and looked sleepily at her older sister. "Boy, are you ambitious this morning. What's the big occasion?"

"No special occasion," denied Kari. "It's just that Tim and I sort of had a disagreement last night, and I want to look really nice for him today."

"Oh." Pam wrinkled her nose. "Mad because you went to the meeting last night instead of out with him?"

"Uh-huh," agreed Kari as she flipped back the sides of her hair.

Pam edged between Kari and the sink and turned the water to cold. "Why didn't he just come along?"

"Come along? To the meeting, you mean? Oh, I can't see

21

Tim at a horse club meeting. I don't think he even likes horses very much."

Pam threw cold water on her face and sputtered as she reached for a towel. "Oh, I think it's worse than that; I think he hates them." Pam threw a gleeful little smile over her shoulder. "But there are other guys who find them quite worthwhile."

"Like Steve?" Kari teased as she sauntered from the bathroom.

"And John," Pam yelled down the hall after Kari.

The name echoed in Kari's ears as she retreated into her room. She had tried hard not to think about John, but his image kept appearing in her mind. No boy had ever affected her this way. Is this what all her friends had been talking about? Was this delightful, heady, and confusing feeling what they called love?

She slipped into her clothes and turned to face the full-length mirror. Kari examined her reflection. She certainly didn't look any different. Weren't you supposed to look different when you were in love? And besides, you couldn't fall in love after only one meeting, could you?

"You're crazy," she told the reflection in her mirror. "You can't love someone you don't even know. You have a boyfriend, and John Garrett would never be interested in you anyway." A funny little flutter in her chest contradicted her.

Kari stared at her reflection. The look was all wrong—too dressy. She pulled an open-stitch ecru sweater from her drawer and slipped it over her blouse. The sweater gave the outfit a more casual look. "That's better," she announced. She wished her insides were as calm and quiet as she appeared on the outside.

Pam propped herself in Kari's doorway. "And speaking of John . . ."

"We weren't." Kari dismissed the subject with a wave of her hand as she reached for her mascara and applied a thin coat to her pale lashes.

"Okay, if not John, although you sure were in deep conversation with him, how about the meeting?" Pam persisted. "Why did you volunteer to take care of the show awards? You don't know anything about that, do you?"

Kari turned to face her sister. "I just decided it was time to stop being a spectator in the club and get involved."

Pam's face wore a puzzled expression. "Boy, did you get

involved. Did you ever think about just baking something for the food booth or helping take entries?"

Kari shrugged. She picked up her books and squeezed by Pam. "See you after school."

When Kari reached the kitchen, she realized she had wasted too much time in front of the mirror. If she was going to catch a ride with Lynn and Mr. Williams, she would have to hurry. She gulped down a glass of juice, called good-bye to her parents, grabbed her jacket, and ran across the backyard to the Williams' house.

Kari reached the driveway just as Mr. Williams was backing the car out of the garage. She waved good morning and slid into the back seat.

Lynn turned in her seat to give Kari a quick appraisal, but said nothing. Kari let her head sink back against the vinyl seat, relieved that Lynn had not questioned her appearance. Explaining it to Pam had been bad enough, she didn't want to go through the explanation again, especially with Lynn's father sitting right in front of her. And she certainly didn't want to answer any more questions about John.

Kari was glad that Mr. Williams taught at the high school and gave her a lift every morning. She hated riding the school bus. When Lynn began a conversation about the coming summer and her job at the club, it left Kari free to relax and look out the window.

She watched without really seeing the newly planted farm fields and the apple orchards in full bloom. Her mind was on the events of the night before.

Why had she taken on a job she wasn't sure she could do? She had never been in charge of anything in her life. Kari wasn't sure she even realized what she had volunteered for until it was too late. She had been daydreaming again and not really listening. Had she sought the position merely to catch John's attention? Well, she succeeded in doing that, if only for a few minutes.

Would anyone assist her? she wondered. Lynn had already agreed to help, but didn't know much more than Kari. Of course, John said he would help. Just the thought gave her a warm glow and a slight smile came to her lips. Kari imagined how it would be working side by side with him, planning out every detail. They would spend hours together, maybe even share ideas over hamburgers at McDonald's.

Kari was completely lost in her fantasy by the time they reached school. Lynn was saying her name for the second time when she realized they were in the parking lot at Brookview High.

Lynn playfully nudged Kari in the arm. "Sometimes, I wonder where your mind is, Kari."

"Sometimes, I wonder the same thing myself," Kari laughed. "But this time I was just thinking about the awards for the show."

"Yeah, I wanted to ask you about that." Lynn glanced at her watch. "But I guess it's going to have to wait until later." She leaned toward Kari. "I'm meeting someone this morning," she said in a conspiratorial tone.

The school halls were already crowded with students by the time Kari got her morning class's books from her locker. She waited in the main hall, trying to get a glimpse of Tim before first-period class. At last she saw him walking with a couple of the other senior boys.

Kari approached him hesitantly. "Hi, Tim." The smile she forced to her lips felt stiff and false. Tim glanced at her briefly before continuing with the story he was relating to his friends.

Kari felt awkward standing with the three boys and yet being totally ignored by them. She didn't know whether she should try to get Tim's attention again or just walk off. Some of her friends passed by on their way to first period and smiled or waved to Kari, who was quickly getting annoyed. She was sure everyone was aware of her predicament and that she looked ridiculous. Finally she had to try again.

"Tim, do you have a minute to talk?" Kari's voice was almost a plea.

His friends moved on down the hall, and Tim's face softened as he turned to Kari. "Maybe we could talk at lunch." He studied her several seconds before he murmured, "I'd better hurry. I'm late for class."

Kari tried to talk to Tim again at lunch. He was sitting at their usual table in the back of the cafeteria. This time he was alone, and Kari felt confident that she could make things right. She sat down across from him and eyed him steadily, but he would not meet her eyes. Usually Kari loved the feeling of sharing lunchtime with her boyfriend. It made her feel special, one of the popular kids. But today was different.

Kari tried several times to start a conversation. "About the meeting last night . . ."

Tim stopped eating and looked up, his fork poised above his lunch tray. "Are you trying to apologize? I accept your apology."

"Apologize? No . . . well . . . not really. I mean, I'm sorry you're upset, but not about going to the meeting. I don't think I did anything wrong."

Tim let out a disgusted sigh. "You don't think it's wrong to stand me up?"

"But I didn't," Kari stammered. "And I'm sorry if it looked that way."

In the silence that followed, Kari thought over their disagreement of the previous evening. She didn't think she had stood Tim up by going to the meeting.

"It's not as if we had a date or anything," Kari explained. "You didn't even say you were coming over to study."

There was another moment of silence, then Tim shrugged. "Okay, forget it."

Kari sank back in her seat. She was the one who always apologized even when she was right. It was as though Tim expected it.

Suddenly he flashed her one of his most radiant smiles. "Hey, the car is working great. I'll give you a ride after school." He reached across the table and covered her hand with his. "Maybe we could drive around for a while and then get a pizza for dinner."

"I don't know, Tim. I'm not supposed to date on school nights, and I have a lot of homework."

Tim frowned. "It's not exactly a date, and besides, I have a lot of homework, too. I figured after the pizza we could go to your house and study." His eyes narrowed thoughtfully. "By the way, is your father going to be around? I could use some help with my math."

Kari relaxed slightly. It was becoming increasingly difficult to keep up with Tim's moods. She was beginning to wonder if having him for a boyfriend was worth the hassle.

Suddenly, Kari was startled by the rattle of Lynn's tray as she set it down beside her. "Is this a private party or can anyone join in?"

Kari made a half-hearted attempt at a smile. Lynn often

joined them for lunch, but today Kari would rather have been alone with Tim. She knew things weren't completely settled with him, and their relationship was being held together by a tenuous thread.

Lynn either didn't notice the tension or chose to ignore it. She carefully pulled her hamburger from its bun and lightly salted it. "Have to watch the calories, you know." She cut a small bite and chewed it thoughtfully.

Kari watched Tim as he watched Lynn carefully examine her next bite.

"I heard your father is going to be managing the club's pool this summer," he said.

Lynn nodded. "News travels fast. But that's right, and I'm going to be running the small snack bar out by the pool."

Kari watched one of Tim's irresistible smiles spread across his thin face. "Looks like we'll be seeing a lot of each other this summer." His voice was suggestive as he continued to smile at Lynn.

A funny little knot formed in Kari's stomach as Tim's inference sank in. She glanced sideways at her friend, but Lynn had stopped eating and was pushing her salad aimlessly around the plate. She didn't look up, and Kari knew she felt uncomfortable about the hidden meaning of Tim's words. The two girls had made a pact when Lynn first noticed boys—they would never go after a boy the other one was interested in.

Lynn's fork clanked nervously against her plate as she tried to regain her composure. "Well...I'll be pretty busy working most of the time. And as soon as I finish at the club, I'll have my horse to work, and I've promised to help Kari with the show awards and..."

"Show awards for what?" Tim questioned.

Lynn ignored his question as she continued. "And I'm not sure yet, but I might be teaching some beginning swimming lessons."

"What awards?" Tim repeated, more firmly this time.

Kari watched Lynn's face turn ashen as she realized what she had done.

"The awards for the Junior Riders' horse show this summer." Kari spoke up. "I'm heading up the committee and Lynn has agreed to help me." Kari looked him in the eye defiantly. "And yes, it will probably take some time. There are a lot of decisions to be made, and I want it done right."

The anger Kari knew was coming came in a single exploding outburst. "Horses again!"

Tim grabbed up his tray and stormed off.

Lynn looked startled. "I'm sorry, Kari. I didn't mean to say anything that would cause more trouble between you two. I wasn't thinking." She pushed back her tray, her lunch hardly touched. "Maybe you can straighten things out after school."

"It's okay," Kari sighed. "I'm not sure it can be straightened out. Tim has a real blind spot where horses are concerned."

"I've noticed," Lynn said. "Have you tried talking to him about it to see why he objects to them?"

"He won't talk. He just gets angry."

Lynn rose to leave. "I don't suppose it would help if I tried to talk to him?"

Kari shook her head and smiled sadly. "Thanks, anyway, but you would be wasting your time. He may be very charming, but he is very stubborn as well."

Kari looked for Tim after school, just in case he had cooled down and still wanted to give her a ride home. She finally spied him walking to his little sports car. He had a friend with him, and it was evident he was not looking for her. She swallowed the lump in her throat and went to the teachers' lot to wait for Mr. Williams.

Thursday and Friday came and went and Kari still hadn't been able to resolve things with Tim. Every time she saw him at school, he was with a large group of friends, and Kari was afraid to intrude. She even tried calling him Friday night, but his mother said he was out. It had taken Kari a lot of courage to make the phone call. She had never called a boy before and felt a little foolish after hanging up the receiver, and a little like she was spying. The rumor around school on Friday was that Tim was seen giving Diane Palmer a ride home Thursday night in his little red Fiat. Diane was a new senior and not at all hard to look at. Kari tried to ignore the rumor. She also tried to avoid the student parking lot on the chance the rumor might be true. In the back of Kari's mind an unpleasant thought took form—maybe he wasn't home Friday night because he had a date with Diane.

By Saturday morning, Kari was feeling rather irritable. She didn't think she had done anything to deserve this treatment.

"Is anything wrong, dear?" Mrs. Stewart questioned, coming into the kitchen.

Kari banged the pots and pans in the cabinet. "No," she grumbled, "I just can't find the right skillet."

She set the omelet pan on the burner with a loud clank and began cracking eggs into a bowl. One slipped from her hand and broke all over the kitchen floor. Tears welled up in her eyes as she stooped to clean up the mess.

"When will Pam be home?" she asked with forced calmness.

"Not until this evening," her mother answered as she handed her another paper towel.

Kari's sister had spent the night with a friend and now Kari needed her. She wanted to talk with someone. In the last couple of months, Pam had become more like a friend than a sister. They still fought frequently, but Kari no longer thought of her as a little kid.

Mrs. Stewart took a wire whisk to the eggs. "This all has to do with Tim, doesn't it?" She looked over her shoulder at Kari.

"Of course not." Kari forced a smile. "I'm just having a bad morning, that's all."

Her mother gave her an encouraging smile. "Why don't I finish up breakfast?"

Kari nodded gratefully. "Thanks. I think I'll give Lynn a call."

She went into the family room where she would be alone. Curling up on the couch, she dialed Lynn's number. She was almost relieved when Mrs. Williams answered the phone and said Lynn had left for an early doctor's appointment. Kari wanted to talk about her problems concerning Tim, but she wasn't sure Lynn would understand. She never had problems with boys. That was what made talking to Pam so easy. Since she had no experience with boys, she would listen quietly and at least look sympathetic. And what Kari felt she needed right now was a little sympathy.

She uncurled her feet from under her and padded back to the kitchen to see her mother putting the omelet and some homemade biscuits on the table, as Kari slid quietly into her chair.

The meal was tense as Kari forced herself to make light conversation.

"So, where's the retirement party going to be this afternoon?" she asked her father.

Mr. Stewart put down his coffee cup before answering. "Oh, I thought we'd already told you. It's going to be at the officers' club at the base. I'll leave the number by the phone in case you need us for anything."

"I think I'll survive for a few hours alone," quipped Kari, throwing her father a wry smile.

"Don't forget, the blacksmith is coming this afternoon," he reminded her. "Are you sure you'll be able to handle all three horses by yourself?"

"I can handle it. None of them are very difficult about getting their feet trimmed. The worst that could happen is that Pam's tubby pony will want to lean on me the whole time his feet are being clipped."

"Well, you know those animals better than I do," acknowledged her father. "I'll leave it to your judgment. If it looks as though you may have a problem, run next door and get Lynn to help."

"I will," promised Kari.

The morning seemed to drag. Although her parents didn't question her, they frequently threw sympathetic looks in her direction, and she was glad when they left to attend the retirement luncheon for one of their engineer friends. She knew from experience that the party could last well into the late afternoon. She was looking forward to the time alone.

Lunch came and went. Kari wasn't hungry and finally decided to give the horses a good grooming before the blacksmith arrived.

She had just led Poco from his stall when she heard a car in the driveway. She knew without looking that it was Tim. The little sports car had a very distinctive sound. Kari felt a mixture of joy and anger at the prospect of seeing him. She quickly put Poco back in his stall and ran to the house.

Tim was getting ready to ring the back doorbell when Kari bounded up the porch steps. She stopped suddenly, not knowing quite what to say. Tim turned around at the sound of her footsteps. He smiled broadly as his swinging strides covered the short expanse between them.

Kari felt his hands on her shoulders as he bent his head to lightly brush a kiss across her mouth. Kari stood immobile.

She didn't feel like kissing him back. What she did feel was a strange indefinable emotion. It wasn't dislike. It wasn't even anger. It was more like she just didn't care.

For two days, Kari had waited to see him and now that he was standing in front of her, she couldn't think of a thing she wanted to say to him.

Tim looked down at her with a puzzled expression and then as if he could read her thoughts, his face broke into a charming smile. He clasped her hand firmly in his and led her down the steps to his car. Reaching inside, he produced a single deep-red rose. "Just for my girl," he whispered close to her ear.

A warm glow spread through Kari as she sniffed the sweet scent. She had never gotten a flower from a boy. Kari looked up at Tim and smiled.

"And now, to sweep you away with me." Tim bowed gallantly and opened the car door.

Kari hesitated. "Where are we going?"

"To the country club, of course." His eyes slid over her in a quick assessment. "Oh, maybe you ought to change first. They don't approve of jeans on the golf course."

Kari almost choked. "What?" She crossed her arms in front of her defiantly. "I'm not going golfing."

"Of course you are," insisted Tim. "Now hurry and change into some slacks."

Kari tried to explain. "But I can't leave right now."

"Why not?" Tim's smile had faded away to a scowl.

"Because the blacksmith is coming. I'm the only one here, so I have to take care of the horses."

A look as dark as a thundercloud passed over Tim's face. His anger was tightly controlled as he growled between clenched teeth, "Not horses again, Kari."

Kari took a step back. "Please try to understand," she pleaded. "It's not something that will take very long. We could do something later."

"But I don't want to do something later; I want to do something now," he insisted. "What time is this character due?"

"About five."

Tim glanced at his expensive gold watch. "That gives us plenty of time for nine holes."

Kari could see Tim wasn't going to listen. She could flatly refuse to go, but Tim would probably never speak to her again. She was beginning to wonder if that would be so terrible. Then she thought of all of the fun times they had together. If she hurried, she would be back in plenty of time for the blacksmith. Kari's heart and conscience played a tug-of-war. She knew she should stay at the house even if it meant endangering her shaky relationship with Tim. As she was about to refuse, Lynn's words of warning came back to her—"It wouldn't pay to make him too angry—he's very popular."

Finally Kari gave in. "Okay," she agreed, "if you promise to have me back by five."

Tim's charming smile returned.

It was a beautiful day for golf. The sun was shining and the temperature was just right. Kari would have been content to walk along with Tim, but he insisted she play, too. She felt she was doing pretty well even though she was taking three strokes to every one of his.

Tim was unusually patient with her lack of ability. Kari wondered if he was trying to make up for being so distant toward her all week or whether he really wanted her to learn to play golf. Either way, she was thoroughly enjoying herself, laughing and talking with him, until they reached the seventh hole.

She made a beautiful tee shot for which he rewarded her with a quick hug and a kiss. But from that point on her golf game seemed destined for failure. No matter how hard she concentrated on her swing, nothing went right. She dribbled the ball all the way up the fairway until it landed in a sand trap just off the green.

They stepped aside to let a group of boys play through. Kari didn't know them, but Tim did. They were friends of his from the club, who teased him good-naturedly about his golf instruction.

Tim's whole mood changed as his hazel eyes flashed in a familiar display of impatience. "You could at least try instead of embarrassing me that way."

Kari was crushed. "I am trying. I warned you I wasn't very good."

Kari pulled her wedge from her bag and took several swipes at her ball. She only succeeded in knocking sand in her shoes.

Tim stepped forward in disgust. He picked up Kari's ball and tossed it onto the green.

"You can't do that," Kari protested.

Tim looked at her and smirked. "I just did."

By the time they got back to the car, Kari was hot, tired, and fed up. Tim had sulked through the last two holes.

He put the clubs in the car and turned to Kari. "Let's get a Coke," he grumbled.

Tim was being so unpleasant that Kari had no desire to extend the afternoon. The dryness in her throat, however, made her realize how thirsty she was.

"All right," she agreed. "A quick one."

The clubhouse was cool and the cold drink felt good in her throat. Tim's anger seemed to subside as his eyes rested on her warmly. "I guess I was a little hard on you out there."

"I was trying, Tim. I really was."

He took a long drink of his Coke before he responded. "If you're going to be coming here with me, you have to make a better showing on the course." He squeezed her hand affectionately. "We'll have to get you signed up for some lessons."

Before Kari could protest, they were interrupted by several of Tim's friends.

As they crowded into the booth, Kari recognized them as the boys who had played by them on the seventh hole. She found herself wedged against the wall by a football-player type with a booming voice.

"How about a game of pool," the booming voice suggested.

Kari caught Tim's arm. "I have to get home, remember?"

Tim glanced at her briefly and then back at his friends. "One short game." He patted Kari's hand reassuringly. "It won't take long, I promise."

Kari followed the boys into a room across the hall from the snack bar. It was a masculine room with wood-paneled walls and open-weave drapes at the windows. Two pool tables were set side by side, and at the far end of the room, card tables stood waiting for the evening players to arrive.

One game of pool stretched into three as Tim refused to quit until he had won. Kari paced the room nervously as she watched the minutes tick away on the large wall clock. At last she tapped Tim on the shoulder. "I have to get home."

He looked at her over his shoulder. "I'll be finished in a minute."

"In a minute? C'mon, you know you can't beat me if you stayed here the rest of the night," chided one of his friends.

"We have to go now," whispered Kari. "You promised."

Tim's voice was sharp as he lined up his next shot. "Later, okay?"

Kari saw the look of determination on his face and knew he would not leave. She clasped her hands together tightly and eyed the clock. Her stomach began to churn as a feeling of helplessness washed over her. She had to get home. She had to be there before the blacksmith arrived. Poco's hooves were much too long, and she was planning to show him the next day. Kari's eyes darted around the room. Her parents wouldn't be home yet, and she didn't know anyone at the club who could give her a ride. Maybe she could call Lynn.

Kari pulled a dollar from her pocket. What had her mother always told her—"Carry change for the telephone in case of emergency." She frowned at the wrinkled bill. Maybe the business office would give her change.

Tears of frustration were burning Kari's eyelids as she walked out into the corridor. Her shoulders slumped as she walked the length of the hall. As she pushed open the door to the office, she was greeted by a warm smile from Lynn's father.

"Oh, Mr. Williams," she nearly shouted. "May I catch a ride home with you?"

Lynn's father nodded. "I'll be finished here in a moment."

"Is Lynn home?" Kari questioned, remembering why she had come to the office in the first place.

Mr. Williams stepped through a door behind him and motioned Kari to follow. "Let's give her a try."

He punched the numbers for his home phone and sat down behind the desk.

"This is going to be my office for the summer. What do you think?"

Kari looked around the small, but nicely decorated room. She nodded her approval. Everything at the club was of high quality, even the summer office for the pool manager.

Kari felt a small pang of envy as she thought about Lynn working at the club all summer. Working here would definitely have been her second choice for a summer job.

My first choice, thought Kari, would be to work for a vet, but that prospect looked rather dim. In fact any kind of summer job didn't look promising.

Kari's attention was caught by the click of the phone receiver.

"Doesn't seem to be anyone home," said Mr. Williams.

"Come on, I'll give you a lift."

As they drove, Kari sat on the edge of her seat, willing the car to go faster. She twisted her hair and glanced at her watch.

Mr. Williams looked over at her. "Are you in a hurry?"

"Sort of. The blacksmith is coming, and I'm afraid I'm going to miss him."

Mr. Williams increased his speed slightly. "Oh, that's why you needed to get hold of Lynn. Too bad she wasn't home. She would have been glad to help."

"I know, but I thought I would be home in plenty of time."

Kari and Mr. Williams arrived just in time to see the blacksmith's truck disappearing down the road.

"Oh, no," moaned Kari. "What am I going to do now?"

Mr. Williams let Kari out at her driveway. "Maybe you can call him later and ask him to come back."

Kari shook her head. "I don't know. His schedule was pretty tight with all the horse shows this weekend."

Kari sat down on the back porch steps and buried her face in her hands. Her parents were not going to be pleased with her irresponsibility. She wasn't very pleased herself.

4

KARI SHIFTED from one foot to another, not meeting her father's steady gaze. She wished he would yell at her. It would be easier to bear than his look of disappointment.

"And now what do you propose to do?" her father asked.

Kari looked up briefly and shrugged. "Poco can't show with his feet the way they are, so I'll have to get them trimmed. There're usually several farriers at a show."

Mr. Stewart's eyes narrowed as he thought about Kari's suggestion. "Having his feet done at the show is going to cost you more money."

"I know," agreed Kari. "I won't be able to enter as many classes."

Although Kari was hoping that her father would soften and give her an advance on her allowance, that hope died when her father simply nodded his head in agreement.

"That seems fair."

When Kari arrived at the show grounds the next morning, her state of mind was less than exuberant. She leaned against the rented horse trailer and examined the threatening sky. The air was heavy; only the slightest breeze stirred to kick up swirls of dust along the track. Her own mood was reflected in the dullness of the bleak day. Her shoulders sagged as she stared across the crowded infield. Pam ran toward her, darting among the parked trailers and tethered horses.

"Here's the show bill." Pam produced a listing of the day's events and slumped against the trailer by Kari. "I don't think we could be one step farther from the ring and still be in the fairgrounds."

Kari nodded her head in agreement. "It looks as though it's going to be a pretty big show."

"It would have helped if we had gotten here a little earlier." Pam peeled the wrapper from the candy bar she was holding and bit into the chewy center.

"In a lot of ways," Kari said bitterly. She pushed herself away from the trailer. "You know how Chief is—if he doesn't want to get into the trailer, he doesn't get in."

"What a moose," said Pam, referring to Lynn's horse. "Maybe we should try a thick board on him next time."

Kari pulled the grooming tools from the storage compartment of the trailer. She rummaged through the hoof care implements and chose a large rasp. Running her fingers over the rough metal surface, she tried to calm the angry churning in her stomach.

"Nothing is working out," Kari said to no one in particular. "And I can't even blame anyone."

Pam came to stand beside her. A frown creased her dark brows. "That's not true. It's all Tim's fault."

Kari knew better. "It was my responsibility to be there. What did I gain by going to the club anyway? Tim is probably more angry with me now than before."

Kari angrily banged the end of the rasp against the back of the trailer. Poco jumped at the sudden loud noise. She regretted her show of temper and reached over to stroke his velvety nose.

"Want me to hold, while you file?" asked Pam, coming around the end of the trailer.

Kari stared at Poco's long and slightly chipped hooves. "If only I could have gotten one of the blacksmiths to trim his feet this morning."

"You could have if we had gotten here on time."

An exasperated sigh escaped Kari's lips. "Only two farriers are here, and they're both busy trying to get their own horses ready to show."

When Kari's father went to get the trailer early that morning, she figured they would have plenty of time. She didn't anticipate the trouble they would have getting the horses loaded. Poco walked obediently into the trailer and stood quietly while Mr. Stewart pulled the trailer next door to the Williams' barn. While Poco had faults, loading wasn't one of them. Chief, on the other hand, was another matter. Lynn's large Paint gelding was known as a trailer fighter. It was a major ordeal every time they wanted to take him to a show. It took both fathers and all three girls to get Chief in the trailer that morning. Kari was exhausted by the time he was tied up and the back doors closed.

"This is never going to work," said Kari, bending down in front of Poco.

Pam lifted one large hoof and placed it on her bent leg. Kari ran the rasp over the edge of the thick surface, trying to smooth the jagged edges.

Both girls were sweaty and tired by the time they finished. Poco's hooves were still too long, but at least the edges were fairly smooth. Kari collapsed on the ground, and Pam leaned against Poco's shoulder.

"Now I know why blacksmiths have such terrific muscles," Pam giggled.

Kari's answer was a groan.

Suddenly Pam straightened up and started smoothing her hair and tucking in her shirt. "Oh, no, look who's coming."

Kari didn't have to turn her head, but only look at Pam's blushing face to know it was Steve.

"What! Sitting down on the job?" he teased.

Kari shot him an evil look.

Steve smiled. "I'm on my way to the entry booth. Anyone headed in that direction?" He looked pointedly at Kari. "Shall I sign you up for barrel racing?"

She shook her head and smiled. Pulling her money from her back pocket, she handed it to Pam along with the marked show bill. "Would you mind making my entries for me? I have just enough time to get dressed before my first class."

Pam shot Kari a pleased look as she grabbed the money and followed Steve to the entry booth.

Kari took her riding suit from the car and stepped into the trailer. Closing the doors for privacy, she slipped into the aqua-blue riding pants and white ruffled blouse. She folded her western jacket over her arm and gathered up her Levi's and T-shirt. When she climbed out of the trailer she found Tim leaning against the car.

Kari knew she looked shocked, but she couldn't control her surprise. "What are you doing here?"

Tim shrugged. "I thought I would come to watch you ride."

Kari was still puzzled. Tim's behavior made no sense to her at all. As she brushed by him to throw her extra things in the car, she noticed his cream-colored slacks, white tennis shoes, and expensive golf shirt.

"Not exactly dressed for a horse show, are you?" Kari couldn't keep the sarcasm out of her voice.

Tim didn't seem to notice. "My old man and I played in the Father and Son Tournament this morning."

Kari couldn't have cared less at that moment, but Tim went on to tell her how well they had done. She turned her back on him and lifted Poco's saddle from the ground.

"Here, let me help you with that," he said, rushing forward and taking the saddle from her hands.

She relinquished her grip on the tooled stock saddle and frowned at Tim as he hoisted it onto Poco's back. How could he ignore what had happened at the club the day before? He was behaving as though nothing had gone wrong. Well, she couldn't ignore it; she wouldn't ignore it. Little dust puffs rose from the infield turf as she jabbed the toe of her boot angrily into the ground.

"Tim, about yesterday . . ."

He swung around to face her. "You know, that saddle is awfully heavy for someone as small as you."

"I lift it all the time," Kari snapped, recognizing his attempt to change the subject. She brushed by him to reach Poco. Pulling the girth under his belly, she secured it tight with the cinch strap. She made no attempt to disguise her annoyance.

"Hey, what's got you so upset?" Tim grabbed her by the shoulders and turned her around.

"What's got me upset?" Kari's voice became shrill, as anger replaced her normal calm. "How about what happened at the club yesterday?"

Tim let his hands drop from Kari's shoulders and he shook his head in a bewildered fashion. "You mean this is all because I played a few games of pool with my friends?"

"Not because of the pool, not because of your friends— you promised you'd have me home in time for the blacksmith."

"Was it really that important?" he questioned.

"Sure, it was important, or I wouldn't have insisted on being home on time." She frowned as she looked at Tim. "Besides the blacksmith having wasted his time by driving all the way out to the house, Poco's feet are a mess."

A look of concern passed over Tim's face, and he glanced quickly at the horse's feet. "Is he okay to ride?"

"Of course he's okay to ride, but if the judge notices, I might get counted down, especially in horsemanship."

Tim raked his hand through his wavy hair. "Gee, I'm really

sorry. I didn't realize. Is there anything we can do?"

"It's already been done," Kari stated flatly. "They really need to be clipped, but since I don't have any hoof nippers they will have to do the way they are." She poured some fly repellent on a rag and bent to rub it over Poco's back legs.

"Gosh, Kari, I didn't mean to cause you any real trouble." Tim stepped forward and tentatively touched his fingers to Poco's nose. "I don't know much about horses. They seem like a lot of trouble to me."

Kari straightened up to dump more repellent on her rag. "They are a lot of work," she said, "but I think they're worth every minute."

Tim nodded in understanding. "I guess it's a matter of interest." He ran his hand up the velvety nose to scratch Poco's forehead. "You see, I thought you were just using the horses as an excuse not to go to the club with me."

Kari's mouth dropped open in astonishment. "Why would I do that?"

"Because I've been such a jerk this past week." Tim looked embarrassed, and Kari noticed he stared straight at Poco's nose instead of meeting her gaze. "Like I said, I really don't know much about horses."

Tim left Poco and began to pace along the back of the trailer.

Kari let out a long sigh. "Don't worry," she said, "I told you he would be all right."

Tim continued his pacing as Kari finished wiping the repellent over Poco's shining coat.

"Where's Lynn?" he asked finally. "I thought she usually came to these things with you."

Kari motioned to the section of the track that had been closed off for the ring. "I think she has a class now."

Tim looked in the direction Kari was pointing. "Maybe I should check out exactly what this horse show is all about."

Kari shrugged. "Suit yourself."

"Are you coming?" he asked.

"In a minute. I have a Horsemanship class coming up."

"What's that exactly?" Tim's eyebrows knitted together in puzzlement.

Kari wasn't sure if he was really interested or if he was trying to make amends. She decided to give him the benefit of the doubt.

"Horsemanship is mainly for the rider," she explained as

they started walking toward the ring. "I'll be judged on how well I ride at a walk, trot, and canter, and how well I can make my horse perform in those same gaits."

"Then how will your horse's feet count against you?" he questioned. "Unless, of course, he trips over them." A look of horror passed over Tim's face. "That really couldn't happen, could it?"

Kari's face broke into a grin at Tim's stricken expression. "Of course not, silly. Poco is very sure-footed. But if a judge sees a horse that isn't groomed well or his feet aren't taken care of—well, he might figure that rider really doesn't know what he or she is doing."

"I see." Tim sounded relieved. "But you might not place as high because of me, right?"

"It's hard to say," Kari answered. "It depends on how observant the judge is today."

Kari felt the warmth of Tim's fingers as he reached over to clasp her hand. She looked up into his smiling face, and he bent his head to lightly brush a kiss across her lips.

"I could always raise a ruckus on the sidelines to distract him," Tim joked. "Then again, they might throw me out for that."

Kari laughed at his teasing. "If you cause enough commotion to distract the judge, you're also going to distract a few horses—mine included."

They had reached the make-up ring and Tim's gaze strayed to the horses in the ring. "When do you show?"

"Right after Lynn's class."

Tim stood on tiptoes to see over the riders in the make-up ring. "Is Lynn still in the ring?"

Kari nodded.

"Great! I'll get to see both of you ride." He started toward the bleachers. "Good luck," he called over his shoulder.

Kari shook her head in dismay as she climbed into the saddle. Tim could be so much fun and easy to get along with sometimes, while at other times, he was impossible. Did the good days outweigh the bad? Kari wasn't sure anymore.

As Tim disappeared into the seats, Pam ran up waving Kari's entry number over her head, but she lowered it quickly as she approached Poco so as not to spook him.

Kari leaned in the saddle so Pam could secure the cardboard numeral to the back of her jacket. As she was leaning, she examined Poco's feet. Her efforts with the rasp hadn't been very effective. Kari frowned. She probably shouldn't show, but she had already paid her entry fees and it was the last of the money she had saved. Besides, she told herself, Poco had worked with long hooves before and had done just fine. He was a sure-footed horse, stocky and built close to the ground.

"Have you seen John?" Pam asked as she finished pinning the number. "Steve said he was here."

Kari shook her head. "No, but you will never believe who I did see." Kari paused dramatically. "Tim."

Pam's eyes widened in surprise. "What's he doing here? Of all the nerve, after he messed up things to begin with."

"I don't think he really intended to mess things up." Kari wanted to defend him. "He seemed very concerned about Poco's feet when I explained the situation."

Pam folded her arms across her chest and looked up at her sister. "I don't buy that for a minute."

Kari spread her hands in a helpless gesture and turned her attention to the ring. The class ahead of hers was finishing and the winners were being announced. Lynn took sixth place. Kari and Pam clapped loudly as Lynn rode to the center of the ring to collect her green ribbon.

"Not bad for this large a show," Kari called as Lynn rode from the ring.

She pulled Chief to a halt beside Poco. "Isn't it great? I hope you do as well." Her blue eyes danced with excitement, and she reached over and squeezed Kari's hand. "Good luck."

The announcer was calling the Senior Horsemanship Class into the ring, and Kari gathered up Poco's reins. She held him back as the other horses pushed into the enclosure, because Poco did much better when he wasn't crowded.

As the last of the riders entered the ring, Kari edged Poco through the gate and urged him into a slow jog trot. Horsemanship classes were always popular, and even though the ring was large, the horses were packed head to tail. Kari directed Poco around a slower-moving horse as she rounded the far end of the oval ring. He was working well this morning, and Kari began to relax as she moved with his easy-going gait. As the tension eased in Kari's hands, Poco seemed to relax, too. The judge called for a walk. The announcer informed the exhibitors the class would have to be divided; the numbers he called would stay in the ring and perform, and the rest of the exhibitors would leave the ring until the first half had been judged. Kari listened closely, but her number wasn't called. She walked Poco toward the gate to leave the ring. Ordinarily she would rather have worked in the second half of the class. It gave her a chance to watch the competition and to see how the judge worked. Today, however, Kari would have preferred to work in the first half of the class. Poco was working well right now, and he wasn't always predictable in the ring.

As the first half of the class began to circle the ring, Kari walked Poco over to stand beside Pam. She looped one leg over the saddle and propped her elbow on her knee.

"Large class," said Pam.

Kari nodded. "What do you think of the judge?"

"Seems fair enough," answered Pam, "but he doesn't miss much. I think he has a little help."

Kari glanced at the ring. "The ringmaster?"

"You got it. So you are going to have to know where they're both looking and just hope Poco doesn't blow it."

Kari nodded in agreement. "I was hoping to get to work in the first half today. Poco is behaving, for a change." Kari pointed skyward. "And it could start raining any minute."

In answer to Kari's prediction, thunder rumbled in the distance. She surveyed the sky and then turned her attention back to the ring. The horses had reversed and were starting to work in the other direction. She watched them as they moved from a walk to the slow, rocking lope of the Western Pleasure horse. The judge faced the announcer's stand and watched each rider carefully. He was a heavyset man of middle age, and Kari couldn't imagine him ever riding a horse. But then, that wouldn't prevent him from judging how well other people rode. He stood facing only one direction and scribbled notes on his scorecard as each horse and rider passed.

It was the ringmaster who really caught Kari's attention, though. He seemed to look in all directions at once and didn't miss a thing. She wondered how much of his observations he passed on to the judge. Kari watched him closely. There was something familiar about him but he had his cowboy hat pulled low on his forehead and Kari couldn't see his face. She watched the two men huddle over the clipboard before the announcer listed the numbers for the reworks.

As the horses were clearing the ring, Kari felt the tension

returning. Her stomach felt full of butterflies and her hands tightened on the reins.

"Why do I always have to get so uptight?" she mumbled. "I hate the feeling."

Kari nudged Poco into a jog and entered the ring behind the rest of the horses. She held her breath as she passed the judge. Poco seemed to have maintained his complacent attitude, and Kari breathed a quiet sigh of relief.

Kari watched the ringmaster move to the far side of the ring. His back was to the rail as he gave the announcer the sign to call for a walk, but he swung around as Poco trotted by. Kari's heart did a flip-flop as she recognized John. The involuntary tug she made on the reins nearly put Poco in a stop. Kari bit her lip to keep from giggling. A sensation like an electric current sparked through her.

Oh, please let me do well now, she prayed.

Poco behaved beautifully. He walked, trotted, and cantered right on cue. When they reversed to work the other direction, Kari was sure she would make the reworks.

The horses lined up in the center of the ring and the announcer cleared his throat.

John crossed through the line of horses as he went to join the judge. He looked up at Kari and winked. "Nice riding, Red."

Such a reference to her hair usually made Kari angry, but coming from John, it was music to her ears. Kari was giddy. She wanted to turn around and say something, but she knew she couldn't.

When the announcer listed the numbers for the reworks, Kari's was among them. She walked Poco to the rail and waited for the class to begin.

A drop of moisture fell on the bright-aqua sleeve of her riding suit.

"Oh, don't let it rain," she whispered.

Another drop fell and then another. Soon a light drizzle was falling.

The other half of the class entered the ring and twenty-two horses and riders started to work for the blue ribbon. The rain was falling harder now and Poco shook his head and snorted.

"Take it easy," Kari whispered. "We're almost finished."

The horses reversed and walked in the other direction. A

couple of horses started to act up as the rain continued to fall. One rider asked to be excused and left the ring as her horse danced and slipped in the mud. Poco continued to plod along. The Stewart horses were not confined to a barn and mud didn't bother them. They were sure-footed in any weather. The only thing that played on Kari's mind was the condition of Poco's feet. Even if the ring were dry, the long hooves would make Poco less sure of his footing.

The judge called for a canter. Poco picked up his lead and started along the far rail. Another horse came along outside them at a gallop. It was clear to Kari, even in that split second, that the horse was out of control. It raced by them, throwing droplets of mud back in Kari's face. Poco shook his head, but never broke stride as he continued around the ring in his easy gait. As they approached John, the galloping horse came along-side again. This time it veered out of control and rammed Poco's shoulder into the outside rail as it passed, causing Poco to slip. Kari lost her stirrup when he lunged to regain his footing. She felt his hindquarters slide under him. Leaning back, Kari pulled his head up to keep him from falling. But as she did so he tripped on his long feet and fell on his left knee. Kari tried to get him back up, but the ground was too slippery.

Fear knotted her stomach. She knew they were going down. Poco nose-dived into the soft ground and threw Kari head first over the saddle. She gasped for breath as the impact knocked the wind from her lungs. Through a dizzy blur, she saw Poco's hindquarters hurtle toward her. She rolled clear as the big red horse flipped over. He lay still for only a moment before he scrambled to his feet and shook his powerful neck. Kari was still a little dazed and had trouble getting up.

"Are you hurt?" A deep voice asked.

Kari felt her head being lifted from the mud and cradled against a strong arm. She looked up into a pair of the bluest eyes she'd ever seen.

"They're blue," she whispered. "I thought they would be brown."

"What are you talking about?" John's face showed concern. "Did you hit your head?"

"I'm all right," Kari managed to say. Part of her wanted to lie with her head on his arm forever, but the mud was cold and wet, and she ached all over.

Kari was also painfully aware that everything had come to a standstill. The class was halted, and she could hear some of the horses stamping their feet restlessly. She saw people crowd behind the rail and gaze at her with concern. For one fleeting second she spied Tim's face in the crowd. An unreadable expression passed over his face before he disappeared from view. The loudspeaker went completely silent, and the only noise Kari could hear was John's beautiful deep voice.

Realizing she was the center of attention, Kari felt the heat of a blush creep up her neck to totally consume her face. She reached up her hands to cover her cheeks, only to discover her face was completely covered in mud. She groaned inwardly and quickly scrambled to her feet. The world started spinning and she stumbled forward. John grabbed her to keep her from falling again.

He was standing beside her now. Kari tilted her head back and focused on his handsome face. His eyes held hers with a kind of amused concern. Kari leaned against him as she felt his arm around her waist.

John smiled down at her and his eyes twinkled with mischief. "I've heard of throwing yourself at a guy's feet, but don't you think you're getting a little carried away?"

Kari pulled herself free from John's grasp. "I'm fine," she snapped. Then she gazed with horror at John's light-beige riding suit. It was splotched with mud where he had held her against him. She reached out a trembling hand to brush off the mess and succeeded in smearing it further. Tears of humiliation stung the back of Kari's eyes. She wished the ground would open up and swallow her.

The ample form of the judge became visible at the edge of Kari's vision. She centered her attention on him, afraid to look at John again for fear of crying.

"May I be excused from the ring?" she asked. Her voice broke and she turned her head away.

The judge nodded his head and smiled sympathetically. "Are you all right, miss? If you need any assistance, John will be glad to help."

Kari shook her head. She couldn't look at John again. She reached for Poco's reins. All eyes were on her and she lifted her chin defiantly as she left the ring. She walked silently, hoping no one could see how embarrassed she was. Kari felt it was the longest walk she would ever have to make.

❧ 5 ❧

THE HUMILIATION of the show ring behind her, Kari pulled the saddle from Poco's back, set it down and threw the saddle blanket over the fine-tooled leather. Mud was caked in every crevice of the saddle, but she would worry about that later. Her muddy boots felt like lead weights as she pulled them off and flung them to the ground along with her riding jacket. Burying her face in Poco's neck, she sobbed until her chest hurt.

Feeling a light touch on her shoulder, Kari sniffed, trying to control her sobs.

"Oh, Pam, I've really made a mess of things this time."

The light touch on her shoulder tightened as she was slowly turned around.

"Pam went to find Dr. Ackers," said the soothing voice.

Kari's gaze moved from the finely crafted boots, over the long expanse of beige slacks, up past the mud-stained jacket to a pair of compelling blue eyes. Eyes that were now filled with tenderness and concern instead of amusement.

"Are you sure you're okay?" he asked as he gazed down at her.

The constriction in her chest loosened as she stared into his eyes. She nodded slightly.

"Even the best riders go down," he acknowledged. "You're not the first, and you won't be the last."

"But they don't make complete fools of themselves. They don't end up covered with mud." Kari stifled a sob.

"So you had a better excuse than most." A small chuckle escaped John's lips. "The sun was shining and the ring perfectly dry the day I bit the dust. No pun intended."

Kari smiled through her tears at his humor, but her eyes widened in surprise. "Your horse fell in the ring?"

"Right in the middle of the finals. Talk about feeling like

46

a fool." John shook his head with remembered embarrassment.

Kari continued to stare into his bright blue eyes. She felt she could get lost in them forever—like floating in a cloudless spring sky.

She marveled at the strange and incomprehensible emotion John aroused within her. She shivered in her excitement.

"You're shivering," he said. "Here." He slipped his jacket off and draped it around her shoulders. Kari couldn't tell him that her trembling was caused by his nearness and not the light rain that still fell. If Kari lived to be a hundred, she would not forget the warmth she felt snuggled inside his jacket with his strong hands clasping her shoulders. Kari was sure then that she loved him.

Not only was he handsome, but she realized now, he was also kind as well. He had not been laughing at her in the ring when he made his flippant comment. He was only trying to help her through the situation, a situation he knew and understood.

At last, and with some hesitancy, John released Kari and knelt beside Poco. He gently ran long, slender fingers up and down the horse's front legs.

"I've already checked them for any heat," explained Kari as she leaned over John's shoulder. "I think I need to walk him out a little, though."

Kari fumbled with Poco's lead, her fingers trembling under John's steady gaze. She found herself wrapped in the cocoon of his arms as he reached around her to release the knot. Without looking away, she backed out of the circle of his arms, taking the lead carefully from his outstretched hand. Still holding his eyes with hers, Kari was reluctant to end the moment.

As luck would have it, Pam did that for her. Kari turned just as Pam splashed through the soggy infield. "Dr. Ackers will be here in a little while—he's taking care of a horse that scratched himself on his trailer when the storm started."

Pam stopped suddenly to catch her breath. Her dark eyes rounded in surprise when they came to rest on John.

Kari watched him dig at the soggy ground beneath the toe of his boot as Pam's eyes darted from one to the other.

Obviously flustered at having intruded on a private moment, Pam centered her attention on her sister and giggled uneasily.

"What's the matter?" Kari demanded.

Pam stifled a grin. "You are."

Kari noticed a smile tug at the corners of John's mouth as he glanced first at Pam and then back at her. She watched Pam reach into the car for the small shaving mirror the girls carried to the horse shows.

Her sister held the mirror up in front of her face. "You have to admit, you look a little weird."

Kari examined herself in the small piece of glass. "Oh, no!" She ran her fingers through her stringy, mud-caked hair.

Pam giggled harder. "You look like something from a grade C monster movie. I can see it now—*Creature from the Mud.*"

Kari was torn between the hilarity of her appearance and the embarrassment she felt having John see her in such a state. As he joined in Pam's laughter, though, the tension retreated from her, and the humor of the situation took over. Laughter bubbled up inside her. She reached over and smeared mud on Pam's rain-drenched face. "You can be my co-star."

John's eyes twinkled as he pointed to the bucket of water by Pam's feet. "Maybe we should help her get cleaned up."

"Good idea," agreed Pam.

John took Poco's lead from Kari's hand as Pam fished the sponge out of the water bucket and threw it at her, catching her full in the face. Kari sputtered as she removed John's jacket and laid it on the trunk of the car. She grabbed up the grain scoop and plunged it into the bucket. Pam turned to hide her face and received most of the water against her back.

"That's cold," she yelped. She grabbed for the bucket, but Kari beat her to it. As she released the contents of the rubber tub, Pam ducked behind John. He caught the full force of the assault with his face and broad chest.

Not to be outdone, John seized Poco's bucket of drinking water. "You're the one who needs rinsing off," he said as he emptied the bucket over Kari's head.

"Have you all lost your minds?" Tim's voice broke through their hysteria. His question was directed at Kari, but he shot a contemptuous glare at John.

Kari sobered and looked up. Tim was holding a golf umbrella over Lynn's head as they stood by the front of the car. Lynn's appearance was impeccable. Not a spot blemished her rose-colored riding suit and every strand of her blond hair lay neatly in place. Tim had not fared as well. His navy blue golf shirt was still intact, but the cream-colored slacks were dotted with mud and his white tennis shoes were no longer visible.

Kari and Pam looked first at Tim and then back at each other. They doubled over with gales of laughter, clasping each other for support.

Tim's eyes narrowed as he glared at Kari. "You're a mess." John stepped forward to intervene. "Now wait a minute."

Kari waved him off. "Look who's talking," she finally managed between bursts of laughter.

Tim handed the umbrella to Lynn and approached Kari. He stopped inches from her. He leaned toward her, his eyes cold as he spoke in clipped tones loud enough for only Kari to hear. "You made a complete fool of yourself and you don't even care. You must have hit your head harder than I thought."

Kari tried to keep a straight face. Tim was so stern. She bit her lip, but the giddiness within her was hard to control. Pam snickered behind her, and Kari was lost in another fit of giggles.

Tim threw up his hands. "I'm getting out of this zoo." He turned on his heel and stalked off, his tennis shoes making loud suction noises as he walked.

Lynn shook her head in bewilderment. She led Chief to the back of the trailer, tiptoeing around puddles and waving the umbrella over her head like a tightrope walker as she tried to keep her balance.

Too late, Kari noticed the danger. "Lynn, don't take the umbrella . . ." But Poco had already seen the brightly colored nylon dipping toward his ears. He threw back his head, snapping the lead rope that secured him to the back of the trailer.

Poco balked a few feet and stopped. Clear of the feared object, he stood quietly. Kari ran after him. She grabbed his halter and led him back to the trailer. Pam pulled a piece of rope from the trailer and handed it to John. Quietly he tied Poco to the trailer gate.

Lynn stood a few feet away. "I'm sorry. I forgot about him being so head-shy."

Kari shrugged. "It's okay. No harm done." She glanced at John, trying to gauge his reaction to the scene that had just taken place.

Lynn's gaze followed Kari's. "What's our new advisor doing here?"

For the first time, Kari was glad there was mud on her face to mask the crimson flush that crept into her cheeks. "He was helping me with Poco," she answered.

Lynn swung her long hair over her shoulder with a toss of her head. "That's not what it looked like to me—or to Tim." She leaned close and whispered. "What's going on?"

"Nothing," returned Kari. "I told you he was helping me with Poco."

"I mean with Tim."

Kari studied her friend's face. "What are you talking about?"

Lynn fingered the ruffled collar of her riding shirt as she stared at Kari's mud-stained pants. "I thought things were better between the two of you. Or at least I thought so at first." Lynn hesitated and Kari moved closer. Lynn raised her eyes to meet Kari's, and Kari could see the concern written on her friend's face.

"Kari, what's really going on? I mean . . . Tim and I talked about you and the horses. He seemed really concerned when you fell. Then, I don't know . . . everything got crazy."

"You mean when he saw us having the water fight?"

Lynn walked to the other side of the trailer and busied herself with Chief. Kari followed.

"Not exactly," Lynn hedged. "Before then. Does he—"

"I don't think he was all that concerned," Kari interrupted. "Did you hear what he said to me?" Kari didn't wait for Lynn's response as she continued. "He said I made a complete fool of myself. Does that sound like someone who's concerned?" Kari sank against the trailer. "Oh, Lynn, I don't know what to do. Everything is so mixed up."

Lynn leaned against the trailer next to Kari and sighed heavily. "Sometimes I wonder if guys are worth it." She smiled faintly. "I guess dating one of the most popular boys at Brookview isn't as easy as it looks."

Kari flashed an answering smile. "It was so easy at first. We never argued, but lately, I'm not sure how he's going to react from one minute to the next."

Lynn nodded knowingly. "At first I thought it was so terrific that you were dating him, but now. . . ."

"Now what?" questioned Kari.

Lynn shrugged. "Maybe he's not as terrific as I thought. Maybe you can do a whole lot better."

Lynn looked out across the infield. Kari followed her gaze to the spot where John was walking Poco. Her pulse quickened at the sight of him.

"He's really cute, don't you think?" Kari asked.

Lynn turned to her with a puzzled frown. "Who?"

Kari nodded in John's direction.

"If you like the type." She tilted her head to one side as she studied the dark-haired boy.

"And what type is that?"

"You know. The magazine model type—perfect hair, perfect teeth."

"I think he's more rugged than that. Magazine model, maybe, but he would be racing across the page in an ad for Jeeps or camping gear and there would be mountains in the background and . . ."

Kari stopped as she caught Lynn's expression and realized her friend was teasing her.

Lynn started to giggle. "Yes, I think he's really cute, too. Does he have a girlfriend?"

Kari studied the ground. "I don't know. In fact, I really don't know much of anything about him."

"Maybe you should find out." Lynn turned to the Paint gelding. "All this talking isn't getting Chief ready to load." She looked apologetically at Kari. "I hope he doesn't raise a lot of fuss again."

Kari left Lynn to unsaddle her horse and walked to the far side of the trailer where John was approaching with Poco.

He tied the red gelding to the trailer and walked up to Kari. She felt uncomfortable as an awkward silence grew around her. Lynn was busy with Chief, and Pam had gone after fresh water, leaving her alone with John.

She pushed a matted strand of hair from her forehead and raised her face to meet his gaze.

His eyes were serious and he studied her for a moment before speaking. "Was that guy your boyfriend?"

Kari simply nodded. It was easier to say yes than to try to explain to John that she wasn't sure anymore if Tim were her boyfriend or if she even wanted him to be.

John picked up his jacket. "See you around."

"Thanks for walking Poco out." She watched as his swinging stride carried him across the infield and behind a group of trailers. She stood staring at the point where his broad shoulders had disappeared, until a familiar voice interrupted her thoughts.

"Is this my patient?"

Kari turned around as Dr. Ackers picked his way through

the soggy grass. He set down his medical bag and bent to examine Poco's legs. "That was quite a spill the two of you took."

He took a good deal of time running his experienced hands over the horse's legs and body feeling for heat and swollen areas. Finally, satisfied that everything was in order, he stood up.

Kari felt his gaze on her and saw him stifle a smile as he took in her disheveled appearance and bare feet.

"Everything seems to check out," said Dr. Ackers. His gaze roamed over Poco's sturdy body. "There seem to be no abrasions and there don't seem to be any sprains. Walk him out a little if you haven't already done so."

He turned his attention back to Kari. "But first, you might want to do something about yourself. You're soaking wet and you're going to catch cold."

"I'm fine," insisted Kari.

Dr. Ackers bent to pick up his medical bag. "Yes, that's what my secretary said when she fell in the lake while boating last Saturday. She's been out most of this week and I'm left short-handed." He smiled at Kari. "And you know how I hate to answer telephones."

A bell went off in Kari's head. "I love to answer phones, Dr. Ackers. Could you use some help at the office?"

He paused for a moment. "Well, Donna should be back tomorrow." He scratched his head and looked at Kari. "I might need someone during the summer when I lose a lot of my student help. Didn't I see a job application from you?"

Kari held her breath, not daring to hope he might hire her.

He rubbed his square chin thoughtfully. "I don't know, though. Some of the work can be pretty hard."

"I'm not afraid of hard work," Kari assured him.

Dr. Ackers went on to explain. "The clinic is a very busy place. You'd be filling in wherever we needed help. That could be anything from answering phones to mucking out stalls."

"I clean stalls all the time. I'd love to work at the clinic. I can promise you, you won't be disappointed in my work." She paused a moment and then burst out, "I plan to be a vet someday."

Dr. Ackers raised his eyebrows in surprise and then smiled. "Well, let me look into it, Kari, and I'll give you a call later this week."

Almost in a daze, Kari watched Dr. Ackers return to the ring. He's going to hire me, I know it, she thought. He just has to give me a job!

❧ 6 ❧

THE NEXT evening Kari did her homework in the family room so she could sit next to the telephone. She would look up from her books, stare at the lifeless brown instrument, and will it to ring. When it finally did ring, Kari spilled all her papers scrambling to answer it.

"Hello." Kari couldn't control the excitement in her voice, nor could she hide the disappointment when Lynn answered on the other end of the line.

"I thought we could study math together. It comes so easy for you, Kari, and I really could use some help."

Kari agreed, and a few minutes later she and Lynn were sprawled out on the family-room carpet with their heads bent over their math books.

Very little was said between them until they stopped for a break an hour later. The girls went to the kitchen to get glasses of milk and to raid the plate of cookies Kari had made after school.

Lynn nibbled thoughtfully on a cookie as she carried the tray of snacks back to the family room. "Are you and Tim going to the party next Saturday night?"

Kari took a gulp of milk. She had completely forgotten about the party. "Tim hasn't mentioned it," she answered. A quick and disturbing thought knotted her stomach as she sank down on the family room carpet. Her voice was filled with panic as she turned to Lynn. "What if Tim doesn't ask me to the party?"

Lynn turned her head to stare at the math problems in front of her. "I'm sure he will; there's plenty of time yet."

Kari picked up the note of uncertainty in Lynn's voice. "Do you really believe that or are you just being a good friend?"

Lynn looked up and a faint smile touched her lips. "Of course he will ask you. You've been going together for almost six months."

"That's what scares me." At Lynn's puzzled expression, Kari continued. "Not that we've been going out for so long, but that we might not be going out any longer. I mean ... things have been a lot different since I started dating Tim. I'm not sure I can go it alone. I know I could never go to the party by myself."

"Sure you could. Some of the other girls in the group won't be going with dates."

"But they've always been part of that group," Kari argued. "I'm not sure I'd even be welcome without Tim." That thought gnawed away at her confidence.

"You're crazy," exploded Lynn. "Where did you get an idea like that?" She grasped a strand of long blond hair and twisted it thoughtfully around her finger. "The two of us could go together. I don't have a date yet either."

Kari was surprised, but she made no comment. They used to go a lot of places together without boys—school dances, group parties, movies, but since Lynn had started dating, those outings had become less frequent.

"It's settled then," Lynn announced, standing and raising her arms toward the ceiling. "It's the day of modern women. We'll take charge and be independent."

Kari laughed as she stood up to join Lynn in her mock salute. "To modern women," she proclaimed. But Kari didn't feel all that modern or that much in control. She was still depressed about Tim's behavior and terribly confused by John's. Had Tim decided he didn't like her anymore or was he upset about the horses? Was John interested or just being friendly to a club member? Kari knew the next few days were going to be nerve-wracking.

Tim failed to call all week, and even with Lynn's pep talk, Kari was feeling pretty low. By Thursday she had resigned herself to going to the party with Lynn. She decided she had been leaning on Tim long enough. Lynn was right; it was time to take charge of her social life. If she didn't fit into the group on her own, then maybe she never really belonged in the first place.

Kari's thoughts were interrupted by the shrill ring of the telephone. She took a flying leap to answer it.

"Hello," she said hurriedly into the mouthpiece. She didn't know which she wished for most—a call from Tim or a call from Dr. Ackers.

But it was Lynn's voice that came over the line. "Hi. You sound out of breath; did I interrupt anything?"

Kari released her breath in a deep sigh. "No, nothing, I was thinking . . ."

"Has Tim called yet?" her friend asked.

Tears stung Kari's eyelids and her throat constricted. "No, not yet," she said. She tried to stifle a sob as the tears she had held in check all week brimmed in her eyes and spilled down her cheeks.

"I'll be right over," Lynn said with a decisive click of the phone.

Barely a minute passed before Lynn's familiar voice sounded from the back hall.

When the two girls reached Kari's room, she gave in to the tears. "I don't even care about the party anymore; I just want to know why he is treating me this way." She sniffed loudly and turned tear-filled eyes to Lynn. "Surely he can't be this angry over a horse."

Lynn's face was sympathetic as she asked, "Do you think he's seeing someone else?"

Kari shrugged her shoulders. She pulled her legs up and wrapped her arms around them, resting her chin on her knees. "Maybe," she said staring at the pale lilac carpet beneath her bare feet. "But why doesn't he tell me? Why doesn't he say he wants to call it quits instead of all of this weird behavior?"

"Do you love him?"

Kari was thrown by the directness of Lynn's question. She stammered as she tried to explain. "Love him? No . . . I don't think so." Kari knew in her mind that she couldn't love Tim. If she did, then John wouldn't affect her the way he did. Kari felt a slight pang of guilt at the thought. Maybe Tim sensed she was interested in someone else.

She let out a long sigh and looked at Lynn. "But I do like him, or at least I did. He used to be so much fun to be with— taking me to parties and dances, making me feel really special."

Lynn nodded seriously. "I've noticed lately that he isn't as nice to you, especially when everything isn't going his way."

Kari was relieved. "Then you don't think it's me?"

"Absolutely not," said Lynn, smiling.

The bedroom door banged open and Pam stuck her head through the doorway. "Hey, may I be on this committee, too?"

Kari's eyebrows knitted together. "Don't you ever knock?"

Pam smiled impishly. "When I think about it." She walked in and plopped on the carpet beside Lynn. "Now, what have you decided on so far?"

"What are you talking about?" questioned Lynn.

"The awards. Isn't that what this meeting is about? Kari said yesterday that we better make some decisions and . . ." Her voice trailed off as she looked at her sister.

Kari turned her head away quickly. She wondered if her eyes were red and puffy and if Pam noticed.

Lynn quickly came to Kari's rescue. She jumped to her feet and grabbed the large packet on Kari's desk. "The awards. Yes, we were just getting to them." She dumped the contents of the packet in the middle of the floor and spread out the pamphlets and sample ribbons.

"Oh! Look at these." Pam held up first one and then another as she examined the various colored rosettes.

"First we have to decide on a style," Kari said reaching for the price lists. She thumbed through the booklet.

Pam raised one ribbon high over her head. "I like this one."

Kari eyed the large rosette Pam was holding. It had three two-foot-long streamers hanging from a large pleated rosette. "It's beautiful," said Kari, "but I don't think it will fit our budget."

Pam looked disappointed as she carefully smoothed the red satin streamers.

"How many do we have to have for each class?" asked Lynn, holding up a single plain ribbon.

Kari studied the show bill in front of her and glanced through the previous year's report. "It looks like we need six for the Halter and Performance classes and eight for the Horsemanship classes."

"That's a lot of ribbons," breathed Lynn. "I think we should go with something a lot plainer."

Pam frowned at the ribbon Lynn was holding. "Not that plain."

Kari agreed. "Something nice, but not too extravagant."

The girls picked out several ribbons and Kari checked the price on each one. After much deliberation, Kari held up the one remaining ribbon. "Do we all agree?"

Pam and Lynn nodded their agreement.

"Then style six-twenty-four it is." Kari fingered the smooth satin. It was a beautiful ribbon, having a pleated rosette at the top and two short streamers. "I wouldn't mind winning one of these at all," she said.

Lynn stopped gathering up the pamphlets to examine the ribbon in Kari's hands. "Neither would I. In fact, I'll take several."

Kari's laugh was lighthearted as she filled out the order form. Working on the awards had been good therapy; it had gotten her mind off the party and Tim and John, if only for a little while.

The next morning, Tim cornered her after French class. "We still on for the party next Saturday?"

He was wearing his irresistible smile and looking down at her in that special way. "I don't know, Tim..."

"Are you turning me down?" There was a note of disbelief in his voice and his smile dimmed.

"Well, Lynn and I sort of planned to go..."

His smile was back in place. "If that's all you're worried about, I happen to know that Doug Bates asked her to go with him this morning and she accepted."

With that announcement, Kari felt her courage desert her. "Then I guess it's a date," she said with little enthusiasm.

The rest of the morning, Kari mentally berated herself for her cowardice. How could she let a boy treat her this way and then go running back to him. He had ignored her all week and then expected her to be available for a party. And it wasn't the first time he had pulled this stunt.

By that evening, Kari was totally in the dumps again. She sat cross-legged on her bed staring at the large manila packet on her desk. She knew she should start deciding on the trophies, but she wasn't in the mood to do anything.

Pam, with her usual burst of energy, came bounding into her room. "Did somebody die? It's like a tomb in here." She stopped short and stared at her sister.

Kari's answer was a glare.

"Really, Sis, you've been moping around here all week and I know you were crying when I barged in here last night." Pam sat down on the bed beside Kari and a look of concern filled her face. "What's wrong? Won't you please tell me?"

Kari stared at her hands as she twisted her fingers in her lap. "Nothing seems to be going my way lately."

"You mean Tim."

"I mean Tim, the job at the clinic, the way Poco has been

showing and . . ." She wanted to say *and John*, but she wasn't sure what she was feeling about him. All she knew was that she felt very attracted to him. Was that a problem? She knew thinking about him all the time was.

Pam got off the bed and walked to the door. Looking back over her shoulder, she said, "Since you're sitting there in your bathrobe, I guess you don't have a date tonight."

"And that's another thing that burns me," Kari exploded. "We're suppose to be going steady and here I sit on Friday night. I should never have agreed to go to the party with him next week."

Kari's tirade ended as Lynn poked her blond head through the open doorway. "Hi, your mom said to come on up."

Kari was surprised. "What are you doing here?"

"I thought you might want to go to a movie." Lynn moved slowly into the room and leaned against the desk.

Pam put Kari's thoughts into words. "Don't you have a date tonight either?"

Lynn rubbed her arm in a nervous gesture and examined the toes of her jogging shoes. "Someone did ask, but I didn't really want to go out with him."

"Who?" blurted Pam.

Lynn paced across the carpet and her eyes darted around the room. "Just some guy. Nobody important." She stopped pacing and glanced at Kari. "So, do you want to take in a movie? There's a new comedy at the theater in town. Looks like it might be pretty good."

"Why not," agreed Kari. She pushed herself off the bed and padded to her closet. "Are you wearing jeans?"

Lynn nodded on her way to the door. "I'll borrow my dad's car and pick you up in a few minutes."

Kari was slipping into her new pin-stripe jeans when the ring of the phone sounded from the hallway.

"I'll get it," yelled Pam, running from the room. She returned seconds later, her face animated. "Phone call," she said excitedly, "and it's not Tim."

Kari's heart leaped as she glanced at her sister. "Dr. Ackers?"

Pam shook her head slowly. "I don't think so, but it's a guy. A guy with an absolutely dreamy voice." Pam stressed the word *dreamy* and rolled her eyes toward the ceiling. "Have you been holding out on me?"

Kari made a face at her sister. "It must be my secret admirer."

She went to answer the phone in the upstairs hall. The only boy who ever called her was Tim, and while he had a pleasant voice, it could never be classified as dreamy. Nor was Dr. Ackers's voice—it was more along the lines of robust.

A funny little excitement coursed through her as she lifted the phone to her ear. "Hello."

The voice that came across the line was exactly as Pam described—dreamy. There was something familiar, too. Kari tried to place the owner, to put a face with the deep resonant sounds, but couldn't.

"This is the High Street Clinic," the voice identified itself. Kari knew then that it must be one of the veterinarians who worked with Dr. Ackers. She had talked to all of them many times in the last several years. Kari held her breath. Could they be offering her a job?

The voice continued. "Dr. Ackers had to leave on an emergency, but he asked me to give you a call. He said if you were still interested in a part-time job to stop by the clinic tomorrow morning around ten."

Kari couldn't believe her ears. "I'll be there," she squealed into the phone. The laughter on the other end of the line was full and lighthearted.

She replaced the receiver with a whoop and turned to Pam. "I got it, I got it." She grabbed her sister, twirled her around and danced down the hall.

Only seconds before, she had been lower than she thought possible; now she was floating on top of the world. Not only would she have a job for the summer, she would be doing something she really enjoyed. What could be greater than working with a veterinarian and actually getting paid for doing it?

The movie the girls went to see wasn't all that exciting, and Kari had trouble keeping her mind on it even long enough to discover the plot. All she could think about was the following day. That night she also had trouble getting to sleep, as she imagined herself achieving great feats in veterinary medicine.

Finally, Kari drifted into a pleasant dream. As with all of her dreams lately, John was an integral part. Together they owned a private clinic and horses from all over the state came to be treated.

Kari bounded out of bed the next morning. Even though

she hadn't gotten much sleep, she felt invigorated. Rummaging through her closet, she discarded one outfit after another. Skirts, slacks, and blouses were spread all over her bed in different combinations.

"Kari, what in the world is all this mess?" questioned her mother, walking into the room.

"I'm trying to decide what to wear." Kari held up a beige wraparound skirt and a plaid blouse. "Do you think a skirt is inappropriate to wear to a horse clinic?" Kari hurriedly discarded the skirt and blouse on her bed with her jeans. "And I don't think wearing jeans would make a very good impression, either, especially if I'm going to be working in the office." She looked at her mother desperately. "This is my very first job interview. Everything has to be perfect."

"I understand," said Mrs. Stewart, picking up a pair of navy blue slacks. She held them out to Kari. "What about wearing these? They're dark-colored and washable, so you could wear them around the horses, and at the same time, they're dressy enough for the office."

"Perfect," said Kari as she snatched up the pleated pants. She picked up a long-sleeved blouse in muted blue stripes. "How about this to go with them?"

Her mother nodded her approval as she began hanging clothes back in Kari's closet.

Carefully dressed, Kari drove the short distance to the clinic. She pulled her car into the parking lot and stopped. Getting out, she leaned against the fender of her car and let her gaze roam over the sprawling buildings of the equine hospital. Though she had been there before, she had paid very little attention to the facilities. It was a large complex set on a wide expanse of land not far from the university. Many of the students in pre-veterinary medicine worked or observed at the clinic.

Kari pushed herself away from the car, took a deep breath, and pushed open the front door of the office. She crossed the room to the desk.

"Excuse me," Kari said to the dark-haired woman behind the counter.

The young woman looked up and smiled a welcome. "You must be Kari. Dr. Ackers said you would be coming by."

She pushed back from her desk and stood up. "Hi, I'm Donna. Come on around." She motioned for Kari to come behind the counter. "Dr. Ackers is just finishing with a patient." Donna walked over to a coffee machine. She poured a cup and held it out to Kari. "Coffee?"

"No, thank you." Kari was so nervous she was afraid her hands would shake too much to hold the cup.

Donna took a sip of the hot liquid and set it down on her desk. "You're going to be joining us here at the clinic, I understand."

Kari smiled. "I hope so. Dr. Ackers asked me to come by and talk to him about it this morning."

"I'll tell him you're here." Donna disappeared through a gray metal door.

Kari looked around her. The office was like that of any other animal hospital. A few comfortable chairs were scattered about the room and a couple of low tables held reading material. Instead of dog and cat pictures, the walls were lined with prints of every breed of horse imaginable.

Kari was studying the picture of an Arabian when the door swung open again. She turned around expecting to find Donna, but she looked square into a pair of deep-blue eyes. Now Kari knew why the voice had sounded so familiar on the telephone. What she didn't know was why he had been the one to call and why he was here now. Kari stood speechless, her pulse racing as she was paralyzed by the piercing gaze of those beautiful eyes. Suddenly, all her problems of the past week didn't seem to matter.

John leaned one hand against the door frame and smiled broadly. His smile was echoed in his voice as he spoke. "I see you survived last weekend." Not waiting for a comment, he stepped forward and seemed to be examining Kari's face. His eyes were bright with merriment, and she knew she was in for more teasing. She could feel the crimson creeping up her neck.

Apparently satisfied with his examination, John leaned against the counter with careless nonchalance. "I'd always heard mud packs were good for the complexion. Seems to be true. However, there are easier ways to get them than sliding through a muddy ring."

John seemed to be waiting for a response. Kari could think of none. He was poking fun at her again, but the only thing that registered in her brain was his off-handed compliment. Her heart skipped a beat at the thought. Of course, he hadn't actually said he thought she was pretty, only that she had a nice complexion. For now, Kari would settle for that.

He was still looking at her, and Kari pulled herself out of her trance. "I'm here to see Dr. Ackers. He might give me a summer job." Kari knew it was a silly statement. She'd already realized that John was the one who had made the phone call.

He smiled. "I know. I'm the one who called you, and you already have the job."

"I do? Are you sure?" Kari's voice was breathless with excitement.

John's smile grew until his eyes crinkled at the corners. "Such enthusiasm." He laughed. "Come on, I'll take you to see the Doc."

Kari held back. "Can you do that? I mean, just walk through this place without permission?"

"Why not?" John opened the swinging door and held it for Kari. For the first time she noticed the white lab coat flapping open over his jeans and plaid shirt.

Kari's pulse raced. "Do you work here?" She held her breath, hoping for an affirmation.

John nodded. "At your service." He made a sweeping gesture with his free arm. Kari preceded him through the door. "Yeah," John continued, "I'm a lab worker, stall cleaner, bandage wrapper, and all around good 'gopher.'"

Kari laughed at John's easy teasing. He seemed to be able to poke as much fun at himself as at her.

They walked down a wide hallway with rooms branching off on both sides. John stopped in front of a door marked *Lab*. "Just a minute. I need to put some things away."

Kari followed him into the room. It looked like a small, well-equipped chemistry lab. She stood in the middle of the floor, afraid to touch anything for fear of breaking it. John picked up a tray of bottles and set them in a stainless steel sink. He stripped off his lab coat and laid it over one of the stools. Turning to Kari, he motioned to the door. "On with the tour."

Kari looked back at the lab. "Do they really let you run some of the tests?"

"Some of the simpler ones," he explained. "The two-year students run most of the others, but Dr. Ackers sometimes lets me run duplicates after hours for practice. You'll probably run a few yourself before long, if you're interested."

If he only knew how interested I really am, thought Kari.

For a brief moment, she thought about sharing her dream with him. She looked at him out of the corner of her eye. He really was very special. It wasn't just his good looks that interested her, but everything about him. Again, she felt the strange little thrill that coursed through her every time she was near him. She was disappointed when they ran into Dr. Ackers in the hall and he took over the tour.

"John has already shown you the lab, so we'll start with the pharmacy." Dr. Ackers's booming voice sounded over her right shoulder as he steered her toward a closed door. Inside was a fully stocked drugstore.

"Almost all medications used for humans are also used for horses," explained Dr. Ackers. He walked over to one of the well-filled shelves and Kari followed. "We have penicillin, cortisone, tranquilizers, antihistamines, and all kinds of ointments." He pointed to the various bottles. "We even have plain old aspirin."

Kari was surprised as she viewed row after row of vitamins, vaccines, and painkillers. "It looks like a veterinarian needs to know as much about medication as a doctor," she said.

"That's right," he agreed, leading the way from the room.

From the pharmacy they crossed the hall to one of the recovery rooms. It was a large closed-in area with thick padding going halfway up the walls.

Dr. Ackers patted the thick vinyl. "This keeps the patients from hurting themselves when they first try to get up after coming out of the anesthetic." He moved a few steps back into the connecting room. "This is where we do the surgery."

Kari examined the six-foot-square operating table. "How do you get the horse up there?"

Dr. Ackers moved to a set of controls and soon the table was tilted at a sharp angle, one side touching the floor. "We strap the horse against the table as he becomes woozy from the anesthetic. When he is completely asleep, we turn the table upright." Dr. Ackers returned the table to its original position. "We get him off the same way we get him on, except that we slide him onto this mat so he can be pulled into the recovery room."

Kari shook her head in amazement. There were so many things she hadn't even considered.

Dr. Ackers led the way through the stall area out to the back of the clinic. "Exercise is very important for proper recovery from foot and leg injuries," he said, leading the way to a large exercise area. "As soon as the patients are able, they are brought out here. Some of the larger equine hospitals even have special therapy pools. We haven't gotten that far yet, but some day I hope to."

"This is fascinating," said Kari. She was so engrossed in watching her dream unfold into reality, she forgot John's presence until she glanced around to catch his gaze resting questioningly on her animated face.

She looked away quickly as a tinge of scarlet touched her cheeks. Her heart beat in double time as she followed Dr. Ackers back to the office.

"I'll be looking for you next Saturday," he said in his loud, jolly voice. He disappeared back into the clinic, the soundproof door cutting off the refrains of the tune he was whistling.

The room had become unbearably quiet, and Kari looked tentatively at John.

He hooked his thumbs in his front pockets and smiled hesitantly. "I guess I'd better get back to work, too. The Doc isn't paying me to be a fixture." He stopped at the door and looked back over his shoulder. "See you next Saturday."

Kari was filled with joyous anticipation on the drive home. The bleak months ahead filled with uncertainties about Tim and no summer job now held the promise of something wonderful.

She let the back door slam shut behind her as she ran into the house. Mrs. Stewart was sitting at the kitchen table grading her fifth-grade math papers. She looked up from her work as Kari entered. "How did the interview go?"

Kari sat down in the chair opposite her mother. "There really wasn't any interview. Dr. Ackers had already decided to give me a job for the summer. He even said I could come in on the Saturdays before school is out." Kari clapped her hands delightedly. "I can hardly wait until next Saturday."

"What did you do today?" her mother questioned.

Kari grabbed a red pencil and reached for some of the math papers to help grade. "John and Dr. Ackers showed me around the clinic. They really have a great setup. You wouldn't believe the operating table. It's six feet wide and tilts and—"

"Who's John, a new vet?" her father asked, walking into the kitchen.

Kari was careful not to sound too interested as she explained to her father, "John is a student who works at the clinic. He is attending the university next fall to study veterinary medicine. I met him at the last Junior Riders' meeting."

Her father seemed satisfied with the explanation. "Now that you're going to be a working girl, you can help with the feed bill for those hay burners." He chuckled as he left the kitchen, and Kari knew he was teasing her. Part of her baby-sitting money had always gone to help buy the horses' grain.

Her mother gathered up the graded papers and took them into the dining room. "Your sister is going to be lonesome with both Lynn and you working this summer," she called back.

Kari jumped up from the table. "Lynn! I almost forgot. I have to tell her the good news."

Kari was out the door in a flash and she nearly collided with Pam on the back steps. "Come on," she said, motioning to her sister, "I have to tell Lynn about the job."

Pam went running after her. "That means you got it. Great!"

Kari found Lynn in the Williams' barn cooling down Chief. "How did he work for you today?" Kari asked as she picked up an extra body brush and ran it over the horse's spotted rump.

Lynn stopped her brushing. "Really well. I might take him to that small 4-H show next weekend. Do you think you might show Poco?"

Kari rested her arms on the horse's backside and suppressed a smile. "Depends on which day it's on. I might be working."

Her friend's face broke into a smile as she realized what Kari was saying. "You got the job. Fantastic!" She threw her brush back in the tack box. "Tell me about it."

Kari unlatched the stall door and held it open for Lynn. "They gave me a complete tour of the clinic today. You wouldn't believe it."

Shooing Chief into the open stall, Lynn latched the door and turned to Kari. "What will you be doing there?"

"Some office work to start, I think. He said they might teach me to do some of the simple lab procedures, too."

Kari wasn't ready to reveal who "he" was. She let Lynn think she was talking about Dr. Ackers. Although they had been friends for a long time, her feelings for John were too new and special to share even with her best friend.

The three girls left the barn and walked across the lush grass of the backyard. Lynn pulled a twig off a nearby tree and absentmindedly tapped it against her leg as they walked. "How does Tim feel about the job? Have you told him yet?"

Kari stopped by a big maple tree and sat down against its trunk. "I haven't had the chance, but I know he won't like the idea."

"That's an understatement," said Lynn. She sank to the ground beside Kari.

Pam was doing cartwheels in the soft grass. She stopped and stretched out on her stomach in front of Lynn and Kari. "That's because he likes to tell her what to do. A summer job was not in his plans for Kari." Pam's voice was filled with sarcasm.

Kari agreed, but noticed that Lynn made no comment as her perfect features molded into a mask that gave no hint of what she was thinking.

7

THE WEEK went by quickly for Kari. Tim didn't call, so Kari had no chance to tell him about the job. He did speak to her briefly in French class each morning, but was conspicuously absent from lunch all week.

Her chemistry class took on new importance as she related it to the work she might be doing at the clinic. She would let her mind drift in other classes, visualizing herself in a white lab coat, working on a tray of specimens until late at night, but in chemistry class she paid strict attention to everything the teacher was saying. He seemed surprised at her heightened interest in the lab work and even more surprised at her many questions.

Even Pam was surprised when Kari came home Friday night carrying not only her textbook, but two additional science books from the library. Kari was always a good student, but studying on a Friday night was out of character even for her.

Pam picked up one of the extra books and plopped down on Kari's bed. "Why the sudden interest in science?"

Kari looked up from the book she was reading. "I've always been interested in science. It's just, now I may finally have a chance to use what I know. John said I might even get to work in the lab."

Pam took a sudden interest in the mention of John's name. "Are we talking about the same John, here? The John with the horses and the gorgeous face and the terrific body?"

Kari looked at her sister with disgust. "If you mean John Garrett, yes."

"What's he have to do with this?" Pam asked. "When did you talk to him? Have you seen him since the horse show?"

Kari held up her hands to halt Pam's questions. "I talked to him at the clinic last Saturday." She glanced nonchalantly out the window. "He works there. In fact, he was the one who called me last Friday."

Pam gave a war whoop. "I knew that dreamy voice belonged to someone terrific. You'll actually be working with that guy?" She fell back against the bed and looked up at the ceiling. "That'll be like not working at all. Wait until Lynn hears. She'll be green."

"No!" Kari cautioned. "You can't tell Lynn. Not yet, anyway."

Pam looked puzzled. "Why not?"

Kari shrugged. "Because it's not important."

A knowing look passed over Pam's face. "If it weren't important, you wouldn't be making such a big deal out of telling anyone. I think John Garrett is more important than you're willing to admit."

"You're crazy." Kari lowered her eyes, but a telltale blush crept into her cheeks. When she glanced back at Pam, her sister was grinning from ear to ear.

"I think he's gorgeous," she said. "Are you going to go out with him?"

Kari slammed her book shut. "I hardly know him. Besides, there are more important things than *gorgeous*." Kari slid off the bed. "I'm going to work Poco. Are you going to ride that fat pony of yours?"

Pam stuck out her tongue at Kari. "Domino is not fat; he's just nicely rounded."

The two girls worked the horses until dark. Pam rode easily on Domino. He was a well-mannered pony, but his age was beginning to tell. She rarely showed him anymore and spoiled him rotten.

Kari worked on trying to keep Poco's head down, but with little success. She was having trouble concentrating on anything but the following morning and going to the clinic.

Saturday morning couldn't come fast enough to suit Kari. She couldn't stop thinking about John and the way his light-hearted laughter made her feel happy, or the concern he showed when Poco fell in the ring. The image of his handsome face framed by his shining dark hair was ever present in her mind.

Kari turned and examined herself one more time in the full-length mirror before leaving for the clinic. She tried to imagine how John would see her. Would he notice that her cheekbones were not quite pronounced enough to be beautiful? She sucked in her cheeks and decided that made her look more like a model, but she couldn't go around holding her breath all day. Kari leaned closer to the mirror. Her ears weren't bad and she had nice eyes, but her lower lip was a little too full. It made her mouth look pouty.

Kari stepped back and ran a brush through her hair. Well, at least that was one thing John noticed. He had even made a comment about her hair.

Even with all of the time she'd spent in front of the mirror, Kari arrived at the clinic several minutes early. She was stepping out of her car when a red and gray pickup truck pulled in next to her. Her pulse quickened as she recognized the driver.

John slid out of the truck and walked over to where she was standing. His hair was glistening, wet from a recent shower, and clung to his broad forehead. The fresh, clean scent of soap drifted to Kari's nose. She couldn't take her eyes off him.

"You're early," he said, stepping ahead of her and holding open the door to the brick-faced building.

"I'm anxious to get started." Kari walked sedately into the office ahead of John when she really felt like doing cartwheels. She found it difficult to keep her voice calm. "This could be the beginning of my whole career."

A puzzled look passed over John's face as he glanced around the office. "What do you mean? Are you planning to be a secretary?"

"Not exactly. I just meant this is my first real job."

John smiled. "I remember the feeling." He took several steps across the room and turned. "See you later." He walked behind the counter and disappeared into the back of the clinic.

That was the last Kari saw of John until almost lunchtime. Reality was not living up to her fantasies. She had not seen a horse all morning, she was not working with John, and she was not making any earth-shattering discoveries in the lab. What she *was* doing was sitting in the office helping Donna update the files. Kari knew it was important work, and necessary, but it was not what she had imagined herself doing. She had hoped for too much, too soon. Kari, she told herself for the fourth time that morning, you are going to have to stop daydreaming and join the real world.

Kari's attention was caught by the slamming of the front

door. She looked up from the file she was working on to watch an attractive brunette approach the desk.

"May I help you?" Kari asked, closing the folder in front of her.

The young woman introduced herself. "I'm Mary Gibson. Dr. Farrell asked me to stop by and pick up these vitamins for my mare." The young woman handed Kari a prescription slip. "She foaled yesterday and the doctor said she needed the supplements."

Kari handed the slip of paper to Donna and turned back to Mary. "What breed is your mare?"

"An Arabian," Mary answered and, as with all horse owners, launched into a detailed description of all her horses. By the time she finished, Donna returned with the bottle of vitamins. Kari carefully listed the item on her bill as Donna had instructed her.

When Mary left, Kari turned to Donna. "Are all the patients' owners that friendly and talkative?"

The secretary shook her head. "Don't I wish. We have one owner who does nothing but grunt to anything I say, but most of the people are pretty nice."

Kari laughed. She couldn't imagine anyone going through a conversation with grunts. However, that's exactly what happened when old Mr. Webster came into the office a short while later. Each question Kari asked was answered with a noncommittal grunt. Donna came to her rescue with a bottle of liniment in her hand.

"Is this all you'll be needing today, Mr. Webster?" she asked, pulling his card from the file and making a notation. The old man took the bottle of liniment and grunted in acknowledgement.

As the door closed behind him, Kari fell into a fit of giggles. "How did you know what he wanted?"

The corners of Donna's mouth turned up as she tried to suppress a laugh. "He comes in every few weeks for a bottle of liniment. I'm not sure if he uses it on his horse's arthritis or his own."

The waiting room remained empty for the rest of the morning, but the phone rang constantly. Kari was kept busy taking messages and making appointments wherever the different veterinarians had allotted time on the big office appointment calendar.

As the noon hour approached, Kari's stomach reminded her that she had not made any provisions for lunch. She turned to Donna. "What does everyone usually do for lunch?"

Donna opened the top drawer of her desk and held up a small bag. "I'm brown-bagging it today. Trying to lose a few pounds before the swimsuit season." Donna patted her thighs.

Kari thought Donna looked fine the way she was, but didn't feel she knew her well enough to give an opinion, so she just smiled.

"I'll be happy to share if you like. Tuna fish, hard-boiled eggs, and celery sticks," Donna said, taking an inventory of her lunch bag.

"No, thanks," Kari lied, "I'm really not very hungry." She willed her stomach to stop grumbling as she filed the last of the patient folders. She didn't feel right about taking lunch from Donna. Besides, if her memory served her correctly, there was a hamburger stand just up the road, although Kari hated the thought of having to sit there and eat alone. Maybe she could just buy something and bring it back here. She liked Donna already, and that would give her someone to talk to during lunch.

Kari had decided on her plan of action and was gathering up her purse when the door to the back of the clinic swung open. Dr. Ackers, John, and Dr. Farrell walked into the office.

John looked at Kari. "Going to lunch?"

Kari didn't trust her voice to answer, so she nodded. She held her breath for that brief moment, praying he would accompany her to the hamburger stand.

"Well, I'm going down the road for burgers," he said. "Would you like to go along?"

Kari couldn't believe her good fortune. "Yes, I'd love to go."

Maybe dreams do come true, she thought as she walked out into the warm May sunshine. First the job at the clinic, now lunch with John.

Kari wanted no intrusions on her private time with him, but she thought she should at least be polite. She turned to the two veterinarians. "Would you like to join us for lunch?"

Dr. Ackers smiled and shook his head. "We're on our way to the university. Thanks, anyway." Kari saw him wink at John as he turned away. Now what was that supposed to mean, Kari thought. He whistled a lighthearted tune as he walked away.

Kari turned and followed John to his pickup.

Sitting next to him in the enclosed cab, Kari scarcely dared to breath, afraid she might wake up any second and discover it was only a dream. She had ridden in Tim's little sports car many times and had never felt this confined. Tim, she thought suddenly—what would he think if he knew she was having lunch with another boy? Kari cast the thought aside. She was having lunch with someone she worked with. That's all Tim would think and that's all there was to it, even if it was with the most wonderful boy she'd ever met.

Kari ordered her burger and fries and sat down with John at a small table for two. His knees brushed hers as he slid into the seat on the opposite side of the table. Kari experienced the same tingling sensation she had felt when he had held her in the show ring. How could such a brief encounter have such a tremendous effect on her? Kari turned her face away, afraid everything she was feeling would be readable in her expression.

John didn't seem to notice. He was deep in a description of a technique Dr. Ackers had shown him that morning.

"It's amazing what they can do with fractures now. Only a few years ago, a horse with that type of break would have been destroyed."

Kari marveled at his knowledge. He hadn't even started his special schooling yet and already he knew so much. Kari read everything she could find on veterinary medicine, but the practical experience she was going to get this summer would be invaluable.

John continued to talk, his features animated as he spoke, displaying the enthusiasm within him. Kari was caught up in his excitement as her own dreams seemed one step closer to reality.

He stopped then and looked at Kari. "Here I am, going on and on. You must be bored stiff."

"Not at all," said Kari. "I think it's wonderful the way you've learned so much already and know exactly what you want to do."

John leaned back in his seat and seemed to be studying her face. "Do you have a dream, Kari?"

She stared into the depths of his deep-blue eyes. "A dream? Yes, but not as well planned as yours."

He seemed to be waiting for her to say more. Why couldn't she tell him her plans? He was so easy to talk to.

Finally John broke the silence. "This morning when you said this could be the start of your whole career, I got the feeling there was more to it than it being your first job."

Kari hesitated. She felt John could read her most private thoughts. "Oh, I think I might want to do something with animals, be a lab technician, maybe."

Kari looked down at her sandwich. Why couldn't she tell him the truth? She wanted to share her dream with someone who would understand, someone who felt the same compelling need to care for and heal animals. But holding her back was the fear that he might examine her ability and feel that she didn't measure up to such an undertaking.

Hadn't everyone so far told her she was crazy? Even Dr. Ackers had raised his eyebrows at her announcement that she wanted to become a vet.

Kari looked up from her sandwich to find his gaze resting intently on her face. "How long have you belonged to the Junior Riders?" he asked at last.

Kari was surprised at the sudden change of subject. "About four years, I guess. I joined right after I got my first horse."

John looked surprised. "You've only been riding for four years? You do really well in the show ring. You would do even better if . . ."

John stopped, and Kari had to wonder what he was going to say next.

"How would I do better?" she asked.

John didn't answer for several seconds. "You're a good rider. You have a natural seat, but . . ."

"But what?" Kari demanded.

"Your horse could use a little work."

Kari was afraid that was going to be the answer. She knew Poco didn't work as smoothly in the show ring as he should, but it still hurt to have John tell her so. She worked the big red horse every night and still he carried his head too high. Kari was afraid it had something to do with Poco being so head-shy, and she didn't know what to do about the problem.

"How did you get involved with the Junior Riders?" she asked, trying to turn the conversation back towards him.

But just as she spoke John stood up to go. "Long story," he said. "I'll fill you in on the way back."

The ride back to the clinic was too short as far as Kari was concerned. She would have liked to talk to John a little longer.

There was so much she wanted to know about him. She did find out that he boarded his two horses at Dr. Ackers's farm and that he worked there on weekends to help pay their board. She also learned that Dr. Ackers was the one who had recommended him to their advisor, Mr. Cooper. The Pinemeadows horses had been under Dr. Ackers's care for years. When he asked the vet if he had a student who might be interested in helping with the club, he had recommended John.

Kari was deep in thought when she entered the clinic office. Donna looked up and smiled. "Did you have a good lunch?"

"Yes," Kari answered simply. She could have said yes, wonderful, I wished it could have lasted forever, and at the same time said no, it was a little depressing, but Donna would never have understood.

Kari didn't see John again until it was almost time to go home. He walked into the front office and perched on Donna's desk. "I'm going to steal your assistant for a few minutes."

"Go ahead," she said. "We're all finished here." She waved the two out of the office.

"Where are we going?" Kari asked, following John through the door.

Instead of giving her an answer, his fingers took her arm with gentle authority and propelled her down the hall into the lab. Kari's skin tingled where his strong fingers wrapped around the sensitive flesh of her upper arm. She didn't want him to let go. He led her over to a funny looking machine and released his hold.

Kari looked at him with a puzzled expression and then back at the machine. She stood quietly and waited for him to explain.

When she didn't ask about the machine, John spoke up. "It's an autoclave," he explained. "It's used to sterilize the instruments for surgery. I thought I would show you how to use it. Since you and Donna got all the files updated today, Dr. Ackers said he will probably have you start in the lab next Saturday."

Kari couldn't hide her excitement. She examined the funny-looking stainless steel machine. It looked a little like an oven, but had several dials and gauges along the top.

Kari watched with interest as John wrapped several surgical instruments in brown paper. He set them in a stainless steel pan something like the ones used for steaming vegetables.

"It works like a pressure cooker," he said, closing and latching the machine. Then he demonstrated how to run the autoclave. "The dials on top control the temperature. When you start working this summer, you will be responsible for washing and sterilizing the instruments used in surgery."

John glanced at his watch. "Do you have to get home right away?"

Kari shook her head.

"Good. Then I'll show you how to run a CBC test." He picked up a blood sample and walked over to one of the microscopes.

Kari hesitated. "What's a CBC test?"

John looked up from the slide he was preparing. "Complete Blood Count. It's like when the doctor pricks the end of your finger. You won't be doing any of these tests. Even the ones I do are just for practice." He returned to his work.

Kari looked over his shoulder. "What kind of tests will I be doing?"

John looked up and smiled. "Stool samples mostly, checking for worms."

Kari wrinkled her nose at the thought and John laughed. "You have to start somewhere." He removed the slide from the microscope and glanced up at Kari. "I'm glad you didn't have any plans for this evening. You can keep me company while I finish these and then maybe we could . . ."

"Oh, no! I almost forgot." A knot formed in Kari's stomach. She clasped her hand over her mouth to keep from groaning out loud. She had plans this evening, but she had forgotten all about them. She was supposed to go to the party with Tim. Kari glanced at her watch. If she hurried, she wouldn't have to keep him waiting too long.

"I'm sorry, John," Kari said, "I forgot I'm supposed to go to a party this evening."

John nodded his head solemnly. "The guy from the horse show?"

Kari averted her eyes from his condemning stare, but remained silent.

"I thought so." He turned back to his work. "I won't keep you then. This can wait until later."

Kari wanted to explain, but she couldn't, not even to herself. John had seen the way Tim treated her at the horse show. He probably thought she was a fool for continuing to date him.

Kari was beginning to feel the same way herself.

"I'd really like to learn more about the lab. I mean I wish I could stay, but . . . well . . . this is kind of a prior commitment." Kari fumbled for words as she tried to make John understand. When she could think of nothing else to say, she quietly walked out of the lab and left him to his work.

By the time she arrived home, she was fuming. She was angry at herself for forgetting about the date, and she was upset at John for being irritated that she had to leave, and she was mad at Tim for being early. He was sitting in the living room talking to her father when she walked in the back door.

"Sorry I'm late," she called.

Tim looked pointedly at his watch before he rose to meet her in the hallway. "Don't plan on making a habit of this, Kari. I don't like to be kept waiting."

"But you were early," Kari whispered, so as not to be overheard by her father. Mr. Stewart was still sitting in the living room, and Kari didn't want him to overhear an argument. She glanced at her own watch. "It's just now time to go."

"Time to go and you're not ready," complained Tim. "You know I like to be one of the first ones at a party. Tell me, Kari, did you do this on purpose to get back at me?"

Kari stepped back in surprise. "Get back at you for what? Tim, what are you talking about?" It seemed to Kari that they had had a similar conversation at the horse show.

"I know you've been upset because I haven't had time to spend with you at lunch this past week. This is your way of getting even."

Kari let out an exasperated sigh. "Yes, I missed you at lunch. No, I'm not trying to get even with you. I told you I was sorry I was late." Kari turned and started up the steps. "Now, if you still want to go to the party, it will only take me a couple of minutes to get ready."

Tim grumbled something incomprehensible as he stalked back into the living room.

Kari quickly slipped into her designer jeans and a pretty shadow-striped, light-blue blouse. She was glad the party was casual tonight, since she didn't feel like getting dressed up. In fact, she didn't feel like going at all.

Pam stood watching her from the doorway. "I guess you don't have time to give me a report on your first day at work."

Kari tiredly brushed a wisp of hair back from her eyes as she looked at her sister. "Not right now, but I'll fill you in tomorrow." Then her eyes began to sparkle. "It was great."

Pam edged in the room. "Did you get to see John?"

"Better than that," teased Kari, "but you're going to have to wait until later for the details."

Kari did a full circle in front of her sister. "Well, how do I look?"

"Fine, but you don't seem too excited about going."

Kari frowned. "I'm not. I didn't have time to work Poco tonight and I wanted to show him tomorrow. And that's another thing. As soon as Tim finds out I'm going to the horse show, the evening will be ruined, if it hasn't been already. On top of all that, I'm really tired."

"I can't help you with Tim or being tired," consoled Pam, "but I did work Poco for you earlier this evening."

"Thanks a million." Kari hugged her sister and went to meet Tim.

The party started out calm enough. Many of Kari and Tim's friends were there. As Tim had told her, Lynn came with Doug Bates. He was a tall sandy-haired boy, a senior at Brookview High. Kari remembered seeing him at the country club the day she went golfing with Tim. She hadn't cared for a couple of the boys she'd met that afternoon, but Doug had seemed very nice.

She watched them as she was dancing with Tim. "They make a nice couple, don't they?"

Tim followed Kari's gaze. "Not really. He's too tall for her. The only place he looks good is on a basketball court."

Kari realized that Tim was still upset about Doug beating him at pool. Kari shrugged. "I think he's nice-looking."

Tim swung Kari in an arc, to be closer to Lynn and Doug. "The only reason she came with him was because she felt sorry for him. He's always following her around at school." Tim let go of Kari's hand. "I think I'll rescue her for a couple of dances, if you don't mind."

Kari didn't. She watched Tim approach the slowly swaying couple. She didn't think Lynn looked all that uncomfortable dancing with Doug. In fact, Kari thought she looked quite happy.

Sinking down into a barrel chair, Kari let her thoughts wander over the day's events. She replayed every wonderful minute she spent with John—every action he made, every word he spoke. She wished she could have stayed at the clinic instead of coming to the party.

Tim broke into her thoughts a few dances later when he dropped into the chair next to her. "You're quiet tonight," he said, handing her a can of soda. "You're not upset because I was dancing with your friend, are you?"

Kari took a long sip of the cool liquid before answering. "I guess I'm tired from my first day at work."

"Work!" Tim looked startled. "You didn't tell me you had gotten a job."

"Well, we haven't exactly talked a lot lately."

Tim squirmed uneasily. "Yeah, well, like I told you, I've been busy." His eyes darted around the room. "So, where is this job? It's not a sales clerk job or something that's going to interfere with our Saturday nights?"

So, Kari thought, she had been reduced to a Saturday night date. She sighed audibly. "No, Tim, it won't interfere with Saturday night. It's only Saturday afternoons until school is out and then it's a daytime job."

"Daytime. Oh, that's great. I'll be pretty busy myself during the day." Tim smiled excitedly and his eyes lit up. "I'm going to be working part-time in the pro shop at the country club. Looks like I'll be spending most of my time at the club."

"That's great. It's the perfect job for you." Kari was genuinely happy for him.

"Where are you working?"

Here goes nothing, thought Kari. I can't put it off any longer. She took a deep breath. "I'm working at the animal clinic."

Tim frowned. "Animal clinic? You typing or something?"

Kari spoke slowly to watch Tim's reaction. "Actually, I'll be doing a little of all the jobs an assistant is allowed to do. I want to learn as much as I can before I study veterinary medicine."

Tim's frown deepened to a scowl. "Don't tell me you're still on this vet kick."

"It's not a kick, Tim. I'm really serious." Kari ran her fingers nervously up and down the soda can. She could feel the atmosphere getting tense.

"Which clinic, Kari?"

She heard the anger in his voice and knew he already suspected at which clinic she was working. "The equine clinic."

"For Pete's sake," he exploded, "aren't you ever going to do anything with your life except daydream and play horsey?" Why don't you get a normal job? Something like Lynn is doing."

Kari noticed several heads turn in their direction at Tim's outburst.

"Why don't we go out on the patio and finish this discussion," whispered Kari, leaning close to Tim.

He stood up abruptly and glowered down at her. "Because the discussion is finished." He glanced at several couples dancing. "I want to dance. Are you going to dance with me?"

Kari shook her head. "Not right now, Tim."

The evening turned into an embarrassing disaster. Everyone at the party knew they'd had a fight since Tim proceeded to ignore her the rest of the night. Several of the other boys asked her to dance, and Kari couldn't help but think they felt sorry for her. At least they were being good friends. She wished now that she had come by herself. Going places with Tim was too unpredictable and always a big hassle. She decided it was time to end the relationship.

The silence in the car was deafening as Kari sat quietly next to Tim on the way home. Her purse strap was nervously twisted around her fingers. She had never broken up with a boy before. Kari hoped she would handle it right and prayed she wouldn't lose her nerve.

Kari couldn't stand the tension any longer. "Tim, about all the arguments we're always—"

"I've got a great idea!" Tim didn't let her finish as he wheeled the little Fiat into her driveway. "My dad could get you a job at the club. He carries a lot of weight over there." He pulled to a stop and turned off the engine. "You could have a really neat job and we could spend more time together."

Kari almost choked as she forced the words out. "I was thinking maybe we should spend a little less time together."

Tim turned sideways in his seat. "What are you trying to say?"

"I'm saying, I think we should stop dating for a while." Kari collapsed against the door. There, she had said it at last. A lump formed in her throat, but she continued. "We argue too much . . . and . . . you want to control everything. You never even listen to me and you're never happy with anything I do."

Even in the darkness, Kari could make out the shocked expression on Tim's face. "Are you trying to break up with me?" Tim slammed his fist on the dashboard. "No girl breaks up with me. I'm the one who decides that. You'll regret this, Kari."

Kari's eyes filled with tears. "I'm sorry, Tim." She opened the door of the little sports car and stepped out.

❧ 8 ❧

THE NEXT morning went much smoother than Kari had anticipated. She picked the trailer up extra early to allow for Chief's habitual tantrum. To everyone's surprise, he balked for only a few minutes. Then he calmly stepped into the trailer and stood quietly while Kari loaded Poco.

"I think he's still asleep," teased Pam.

Kari suppressed a smile. "If that's the case, then we'll load him at the crack of dawn every time we show."

Lynn wasn't amused by their teasing. She had been in a sour mood all morning.

"What's bothering you?" Kari asked, concerned that she may have been the cause of Lynn's mood.

Lynn just grumbled and climbed into the car.

The drive to the 4-H show was equally uneventful. They found a parking spot close to the ring and unloaded the horses. Kari tied Poco to the back of the trailer and hummed as she brushed him out. Lynn sat on the trunk of the car, tapping her entry number irritably against the metallic surface. She slid down from her perch and grabbed her riding suit from the car. She turned around to glare at Kari. "Why are you so happy this morning?"

Kari stopped her humming. She threw her hands over her head, executed a ballet turn and smiled at Lynn. "Because it's a beautiful day. The sun is shining, Poco's feet are trimmed, I finally stood up for myself and—"

"And John is here," Pam whispered over her shoulder.

"And . . . what?" Kari stopped her twirling and looked at Pam.

Her sister nodded. "I saw him over by the entry booth talking to Steve."

Kari casually turned and craned her neck to peer at the table where they were taking the entries. She felt deflated when she didn't see his dark head. Perhaps Pam was mistaken.

Kari turned back to Poco. Whether John was here or not was incidental. If Tim was any indication of how boys behaved, John would probably still be angry with her anyway.

She saddled up her big sorrel gelding and walked him to the make-up ring. She folded down the bottoms of her lime-green riding pants and hoisted herself into the saddle. Turning Poco into the ring, her heart skipped a beat. There was John on the far side of the ring, working out a sorrel mare. Kari pretended not to see him as she nudged Poco into a jog along the rail. She had circled the ring once when a horse came alongside and slowed its pace to match Poco's.

"Don't you speak to your friends anymore?"

Kari looked over at John's smiling face and her heart turned over. "I didn't know you were showing today," he said, pulling his horse to a halt. "Good thing the sun is shining."

Kari ignored his teasing, but was secretly glad he no longer seemed angry with her. "I don't remember you mentioning being here either." Kari pulled her eyes away from his handsome face as she stopped Poco. "I see you ride a sorrel, too."

John reached over and patted his mare on the neck. "I guess I have a weakness for redheads." He looked pointedly at Kari's hair and she blushed crimson.

Why did she always let John's teasing get to her? She silently cursed the fair skin that let her blush so easily. Why couldn't she just think of a clever reply?

"I have to warm up Poco," she said, and moved on ahead of him. All she could think about was getting away from his piercing gaze. She felt he could see much more than she wanted him to know.

John didn't try to catch up with her, but worked his mare slowly behind. Kari knew he was watching her. Finally she left the ring. Her nerves were so much on edge that she was transmitting her turmoil to Poco.

When Kari reached the trailer, Lynn was still leaning against the car, her face expressionless. Finally Kari approached her. "Did I do something wrong?"

Lynn shook her head. She handed Kari the entry number and turned her back for Kari to pin it on. "Want to get a Coke?" Lynn said at last.

The girls purchased their Cokes and walked over to look at the awards to be given at the show. Lynn edged along behind

Kari. "How did things go between you and Tim last night?"

Kari leaned over to take a closer look at the High Point trophy. "We had a fight, as I'm sure everyone at the party knows."

Lynn lost interest in the awards. "Did you get things straightened out?" She walked aimlessly along the front of the table. "I noticed you weren't saying much when you left. Does he know you're at a horse show today?"

Kari moved down the table to check out the ribbons. "The subject didn't come up."

Lynn followed her. "Then what was the fight about?"

Kari looked exasperated. She was tired of all the questions about Tim. "My job," she answered. "He thinks it's weird for a girl to be working with a veterinarian. He wants to know why I don't have a normal job like you."

"He said that?" Lynn's head snapped up. "What else did he say?"

"Oh, I don't know." Kari brushed the question aside. She wanted to forget about Tim and last night.

Lynn walked away and Kari turned her attention back to the awards. The 4-H show was about the same size the Junior Riders' show would be. Kari was making mental notes on the awards when she felt the warm breath against her neck.

"Picking out the ones you plan to win?" asked the teasing voice near her ear.

Kari jumped. She stepped backward, catching John's toe with the heel of her boot.

"Ouch," he cried, grabbing his toe and hopping back. He made a comical scene, but Kari was mortified. Why was she such a klutz whenever he was around? She turned her attention back to the table to cover her confusion. "Actually, I'm trying to get an idea of what to order for our own show. I don't have any experience with this kind of thing. I thought this would give me an idea. They have to be ordered pretty soon. Mr. Cooper gave me a folder, but I don't know . . ." Kari knew she was rambling on, that she was speaking too fast, but the words kept tumbling out of her mouth uncontrolled. "We've chosen the style of ribbons."

John held up his hand in a halting motion. "Whoa!" His face broke into a broad grin, and he leaned against the table next to her. "You said we. Does that mean you've found someone to help you?"

"Lynn and Pam, but they know about as little as I do." She looked him boldly in the eye. "So, I'm open for offers." She couldn't believe what she was saying. The words just spilled out. Kari lowered her eyes to the open neck of his Western shirt. What if he rejected the idea? She would really feel dumb.

"I'll be glad to help," he was saying. "Didn't I tell you that's what an advisor is supposed to do?"

Kari was both relieved and disappointed, relieved that he was going to help but disappointed that he was only doing it as part of his duty.

Kari and John spent the next hour hunched over the hood of the Stewarts' car, with the show bill and pamphlets spread out before them. By the time the Performance classes were due to start, they had chosen the trophies for the club's show.

Kari had been so intent on making the right decisions that she had been able to ignore John's closeness. Now that the task was complete, she became painfully aware of his dark head just inches from her own, his shoulder lightly brushing her own. The light spicy smell of his after-shave drifted to her nostrils. Her eyes focused on the strong muscles of his forearm visible below his rolled-up sleeves. She watched his long slender fingers as he finished listing the style numbers on a slip of paper. Kari felt the strongest desire to reach out and touch him. Straightening quickly, she forced herself to back away.

John looked up when she backed away. "I'll let you take it from here." He gathered up the papers and held them out to her.

She was stuffing them back into the envelope when Lynn rode up on Chief and dismounted. She looked from John to Kari and back again. "Seems like I've been seeing a lot of you around our trailer lately," she teased. A smile spread across her pretty features; the first one Kari had seen all day.

"The scenery is better over here," John flipped back at her. "Where else could I find a blond, a brunette, and a redhead all in one spot?"

He smiled at Kari before he stepped forward and grabbed the headstall of Chief's bridle. Examining the bit, he asked Lynn, "Does he toss his head at all when you pull back on the reins?"

"All the time lately," she answered. "I think that's what knocked me down to sixth place the last show."

John adjusted the headstall so that the bit fit differently in

Chief's mouth. "I'm not surprised. You were gagging him with the bit that tight." John stood back from the big Paint gelding. "That should take care of the problem."

He turned to Kari. "I'd better go. I have a date with a redhead for the ring." He touched the tip of his cowboy hat in a mock gesture and walked away.

Lynn looked surprised. "What was all that about?"

"Nothing, he just likes sorrel horses, and I'm sure you already know he's a big tease."

Lynn laughed. "With you anyway." She observed the packet in Kari's hands. "Oh, that's it. He was helping you with the trophies. I thought maybe there was another reason."

"No, just fulfilling his job as a junior advisor."

The rest of the day didn't go as well for Kari. She leaned against the slatted rails of the ring to watch her sister show Poco in Junior Horsemanship. He kept tossing his head whenever another horse cut too close in front of him and he even missed one of his leads. Kari knew she wouldn't be taking home any ribbons today. That fact didn't bother her nearly as much as having John think she didn't know how to train her horse. He was sitting astride his sorrel mare waiting for the next class. Several times Kari glanced up to catch him looking in her direction, but he would quickly turn his attention back to the ring.

Kari's class went almost as poorly as Pam's. Poco threw his head at every provocation. He was working too fast, but at least he picked up his leads and performed all his gaits. Kari was pleasantly surprised when the places were announced and her number was among them. It was only a sixth place, but Kari was happy to accept the green satin ribbon.

She was leaning against the trailer later, running her fingers over its shiny surface when John appeared. She watched his tall, lean form cross the short grassy distance between them. He rested one hand on the side of the trailer above Kari's head so that he was leaning over her.

"Happy with the ribbon, huh?" It was more of a statement than a question.

Kari smiled up at him. "Not as good as a first place, but it will do for now. I noticed you took a couple of firsts." His nearness was making her nervous, and she felt she had to put some distance between them. Ducking under his arm, she moved Poco from the back of the trailer so Lynn could load Chief.

The pretty blonde had gotten several of her admirers to help with the loading. It was a smart move as the big Paint was up to his old tricks. Kari watched for several minutes while the spotted gelding lunged and dived and fought getting into the trailer.

While Kari had been watching Chief, John had led Poco a little distance from the trailer. She watched while John trotted Poco in a small circle. Then he dismounted and made various moves at Poco's head, first with his hand, then with the reins, and finally with a heavy stick. As John picked up the wooden object, Poco rolled his eyes and flattened his ears. He tried to pull away, but John held him securely.

Kari was furious. She ran up to John and grabbed the reins from his hand. "What do you think you're doing?"

John caught Kari by the shoulders. "Calm down. I wasn't hurting him. I was just trying to find out something."

Kari shrugged out of John's hold. "And did you find it out?" Kari knew she was yelling, but she couldn't help herself.

"Yes," he said softly, "I'm afraid I have." John sighed audibly and reached out a hand to stroke Poco's neck. The horse immediately calmed down under his gentle touch. John looked at Kari as he continued to soothe the horse. "Your horse has been mistreated."

Kari frowned. She wasn't sure what he meant. All she knew was that she had given Poco the very best care she knew how since she had gotten him a year ago. "I don't think I've ever mistreated any of my horses."

"Not by you, by a former owner probably—I don't know." He took the reins from Kari's hands and led Poco back to the trailer. He slipped the bridle from the horse's head and fastened on the halter and lead. John turned to her sadly. "Poco has been beaten, badly." When Kari made no reply, he went on. "I've been watching him in a number of situations today. He is fine with your hands around his head, even with the reins or a whip, but anything large makes him crazy."

Kari's eyes filled with tears. "I've never hit him, not even with a riding crop."

"I already said I know it wasn't you." He took off his cowboy hat and ran his fingers through his dark hair in an agitated gesture. "You told me you bought Poco about a year ago. You also said he was seven years old. That leaves a lot of time for someone else to have messed him up good."

"But he's gotten excellent care from me. Shouldn't that make a difference?" Kari's eyes pleaded with John to tell her everything would be fine.

John shook his head sadly. "A little, maybe. A horse is like any animal that's been mistreated, or even a person. He's lost his trust."

Kari leaned her forehead against Poco's cheek and stroked his ears. "And if I can't rebuild his trust?"

"Then he'll be worthless as a show horse or for any kind of pleasureable riding."

Kari swung around to face him, her fists balled at her sides. "You don't know what you're talking about. Poco's a good riding horse." Tears streamed down her face. "You think you're such an expert, but you only rode him for a few minutes. How could you tell anything?" Kari turned her back. "Just go away and leave me alone."

Lynn came to stand by the side of the trailer. Her eyes were big and round and her mouth was hanging open. Kari ignored her as she pushed by to load Poco in the trailer. She glanced back at the spot where John had been standing. He was gone, and Kari felt a sharp constriction in her chest. What had she done?

Kari dragged herself through the following week. She knew what John had told her was true. It had been at the back of her own mind for several months. She just hadn't wanted to face the fact.

She flopped on her bed and stared at the ceiling. Never could she remember feeling quite so miserable. The words she had hurled at John kept echoing in her mind and she realized the last thing she wanted was for him to go away and leave her alone. Kari felt hot tears on her cheeks. She buried her face in her pillow and cried herself to sleep again.

When Saturday arrived, Kari drove to the clinic, rehearsing several speeches to say to John on the way. Somehow she had to let him know that she had spoken in anger, that she hadn't really meant what she'd said.

All morning she waited to speak to him. Every time the door to the office swung open she would glance up hopefully, but John never appeared.

"Are you looking for someone?" Donna asked finally. "You've been on edge all morning."

"Uh, well . . . yes." Kari hedged. "Have you seen John?"

Donna was busy setting out her hard-boiled eggs and celery sticks. "He's off this weekend." She folded her bag neatly, and Kari waited tensely for her to continue. "I think he's taking some tests at the university or something. I'm not really sure."

Kari saw her dream crumble. She had hoped to make things right between them this morning. Her visions of them having lunch and working side by side in the lab all faded away. She picked up the billing book and began posting costs.

"Aren't you eating?" asked Donna.

"I'm not very hungry." The truth was, her stomach was in knots. All her planned speeches were wasted. She wouldn't get to see John until the following weekend.

Kari dreaded the coming week. To her, it was hours of time she had to get through before she could see John again. To make matters worse, it was the last week of school, and Kari wasn't sure she was going to be able to concentrate on her finals.

She finished them on Thursday and debated whether she should go to the clinic the next day. Dr. Ackers wasn't expecting her until Saturday and she didn't want John to think she was coming to see him. She decided she would wait.

Her day off was spent giving Poco an extra long workout. She was planning on going to another show and she wanted him working his best. Somehow, she had to show John that Poco wasn't worthless as a show horse.

When she finished with her horse, Kari went to work on herself. She spent an extra long time doing her hair and trying new hairstyles. She even did her nails and coated them with a peach-colored gloss.

By the time Kari arrived at the clinic Saturday morning, she felt really good. Poco was working much better and she was sure John would forgive her for her outburst. Marching through the front door, she said hello to Donna and went straight through to the lab. Not finding John, Kari continued down the hall, checking the operating room and the recovery rooms. She found him in the pharmacy getting some ointment for one of the patients. Kari stopped just inside the door and placed her hands on her hips.

"Where were you last weekend?" She didn't intend the question to sound so much like an accusation.

John raised his eyebrows in surprise. He set the ointment on the table and took a couple of steps closer. His eyes sparkled with mirth and his face relaxed in a smile. "Did you miss me?" he asked in a teasing tone.

Kari turned her back so her blush wouldn't give her away. John reached around her and captured her chin in his strong hand. He forced her face upward so she had to look him in the eye.

"I asked if you missed me?" His voice was still teasing, but his eyes were sending a different message. "Aren't you the same girl who told me to get lost?" He was looking at her with such an intensity that Kari looked away, confused. Was he making fun of her or was he flirting?

Kari pulled away and tried to steady her voice. "It's just that you promised to show me some of the lab tests and then you weren't even here."

"I'm sorry," he apologized. "I forgot I had another commitment." His voice had lost its humor. He brushed against Kari as he hurriedly left the room.

Kari stamped her foot in frustration. That wasn't how she'd planned their conversation. She wanted to let him know she hadn't meant what she'd said at the horse show.

Kari saw very little of John during her first full week of work. She spent the mornings in the office helping Donna with appointments and billings. The afternoons were mostly routine. She washed and sterilized the surgical instruments and ran errands for the doctors. She wasn't allowed to fill prescriptions, but was allowed to get the various medications and vitamins that were already packaged.

By her second week, she found her days split between the lab, pharmacy, and office. Kari loved the work and found she was learning something new every day. She never realized there was so much to know. The veterinarians were impressed by her enthusiasm and taught her many of the basic procedures during their spare moments. Even Dr. Ackers had become convinced that she was serious about a career in veterinary medicine.

The one thing that kept Kari from being truly happy was John. She rarely saw him except for a brief glimpse in the morning or right before she left in the evening. He always smiled and waved, but they hadn't talked since the day in the pharmacy. So she was completely taken by surprise when he walked in the lab on Saturday afternoon.

Kari was just taking some sterile instruments from the autoclave when he walked up behind her. She almost dropped the instruments in her excitement. She set the stainless steel pan on the lab counter and stared at his smiling face.

"Where have you been lately?" she asked, trying to control the tremor in her voice.

"I believe we've had this conversation before," he teased. He leaned closer and Kari could feel his warm breath on her face. His closeness was doing strange things to her insides again.

"Did you miss me?" he whispered.

A smile touched her lips and she nodded.

John put on a lab coat and picked up several samples. He set them down on the table by the microscope. "Did you learn how to do the tests while I was gone?" he asked, turning to look at Kari.

She grabbed another lab coat and slipped it on over her jeans and cotton blouse. "I think I'm going to learn right now."

"You bet." John prepared a slide. "But you'll still have to be checked out by one of the veterinarians before you can do them on your own." He carefully placed the slide under the microscope. "These are some samples we took in the field this morning."

Kari's mind raced. He'd been working with the field veterinarians for the last two weeks. He hadn't been trying to avoid her at all. Kari's heart sang as she leaned over the lab table and tried to concentrate on what John was showing her.

"What are we looking for?" she asked. "Worms?"

"Several different kinds of worms," he answered. "Some you can see with the naked eye, others are much smaller. They all can do a lot of damage if left untreated."

Afternoon drifted into evening before they finished. John carefully read each test result, and Kari listed them on a lab sheet bearing the patient's name. "Come on, let's put these in the files," he said when they had finished.

John switched off the lab lights and stepped into the hall. The clinic was quiet except for the stall area where the veterinarian on duty was checking out some of the patients. John draped his arm lightly over Kari's shoulders and shortened his long strides as they walked to the office. Her head was reeling. She wanted to stay wrapped up in his arm forever, but when they reached the office, he removed his arm to hold open the door.

Kari's fingers trembled as she slipped the lab reports into the various patient folders. In the quiet of the office, she could almost believe her fantasy was a reality. It was no longer the High Street Clinic, but one that she and John had for their own practice.

Her reverie was broken by John's deep voice close to her shoulder. "I believe you just included old Mr. Webster's liniment bill in with the lab reports for the Pinemeadows horses."

Kari snapped to attention, embarrassed at being caught in such a silly mistake, and all because she was daydreaming. She hurriedly removed the offending bill and flipped the folder closed. Turning quickly to refile the records, she collided with John. He had pulled the folders for the Grand View Arabian Farms and the collision sent papers in all directions.

"Oh, no," Kari gasped and bent to retrieve the scattered records.

John stooped beside her, carefully sorting test results and information forms for different patients. They both grabbed for the same folder and their fingers touched. A shock wave sparked up Kari's arm. She grasped the folder with a kind of desperation as she turned her eyes up to John's face. He had an odd look in his eyes and Kari knew he was going to kiss her. Her heart was pounding so loud, she was sure John could hear it, too. His lips brushed hers and it was unlike anything Kari had ever experienced. She stared into his long-lashed blue eyes and sighed softly. More than anything at that moment, she wanted him to kiss her again.

The door to the back of the clinic banged open. A middle-aged man in green surgical clothes walked into the reception area and leaned heavily on the counter.

"You kids still here?" Dr. Farrell eyed Kari and John.

Kari felt her face flush. She was sure he could tell what had just happened.

His eyes moved to the few papers still scattered on the floor. "A small accident with the files, huh?" He directed his next statement at John. "Make sure you get all of the papers put in the right places. It's very important." He glanced at the folder still held between them and chuckled.

Kari released it immediately and reached for the last remaining file. Awkwardly she held the folders to her chest and walked to the file cabinet. John followed with his folders. He looked at Kari and smiled quickly before lowering his head back to the file drawer. She suppressed a giggle and glanced over her shoulder at Dr. Farrell.

He was leaning patiently against the counter, arms folded, waiting for them to finish the task.

John slammed the filing drawer shut. "I guess I'll see you next week."

"Aren't you showing tomorrow?" Kari knew she sounded disappointed, but she couldn't help it.

"Can't. I have to work." He stared at her for a long moment until Dr. Farrell cleared his throat.

"Are you two about finished so I can lock up the front?"

"Right away." Kari grabbed her purse from Donna's bottom desk drawer and followed John out the front door.

He walked her to her mother's car and opened the door. "See ya."

"Yeah." Kari stood looking into his face. Even in the dark she could make out his handsome features.

John drummed his fingers against the door frame. "Well, I guess I'd better get going." He took a step back.

Kari climbed into the car. On the short drive home, she relived every second of John's kiss.

9

THE NEXT morning, Kari lowered the ramp on the trailer. She frowned as she examined the weathered boards.

"Do you think this thing is safe?" She jabbed at the floor boards with the toe of her boot.

Lynn threw her stable blanket on the ground in disgust. "Don't be so picky."

"Don't snap at me. I'm not the one who forgot to reserve the trailer, remember."

Lynn glared at Kari. "I told you, I had to work late. I did the best I could." Lynn stormed off.

Kari looked after her and sighed. What was going on? Lynn had been her closest friend since Kari's family had moved next door five years ago. Now she rarely saw her except on weekends, and the last couple of times, all they did was pick on each other and argue.

Kari jumped up and down in the trailer. "Well, I guess the floor is pretty sound," she said to no one in particular, "but that ramp looks a little rickety." She stepped out of the trailer. Walking around to the side, she kicked the tire. Satisfied the trailer was safe, Kari went to get Poco.

He was standing quietly in his stall when Kari entered the barn. She greeted him with a cheerful hello and affectionately slapped his neck.

"Come on, big fella. Your carriage awaits." Kari fastened a lead rope to Poco's halter and led him from the stall. She cross-tied the rope and fetched her box of brushes from the tack room.

"Could you use a hand?" Pam asked, entering the barn.

Kari tossed her a body brush. "Extra hands are always appreciated."

The two sisters worked in silence for several minutes. The

only sound in the barn was the swish of the brushes over the sleek red hide.

At last Kari asked, "Have you talked to Lynn lately?"

Pam stopped her brushing and looked up. "Sure. Why?"

"No reason, it just seems things are different between us. Maybe it's the long hours she has been working."

"What long hours? She gets home before you do, except when there's a pool party." Pam dropped the brush into the storage box and picked up the mane comb. "I think it's her social life that's wearing her out." Pam walked to the rear of the horse and pulled his tail to one side. "Looks like his tail could use a little thinning, Sis."

Kari wasn't listening. Her thoughts were still on Lynn. "Was there a pool party Thursday night?"

Pam's eyebrows knitted together in thought. "I think so. In fact, I know so." She tapped the metal comb on her forefinger. "Because Lynn had a date that night."

Kari looked up in surprise. "What? She said she had to work. That's why she didn't get a trailer reserved."

Pam shrugged. "That's just what her mom said."

Kari was more puzzled than before. She picked up Poco's stable blanket and tossed it to her sister who spread the royal blue cover over the horse's back and fastened it snugly. Then Pam grabbed the box of grooming tools, and Kari untied Poco.

She brushed her hair back from her damp forehead. "Let's get him loaded." The girls walked Poco across the backyard. Before the trailer was in view, they could hear the ruckus.

"Sounds like Lynn is trying to load Chief," Kari said in explanation of the racket.

Pam nodded her agreement.

The girls could see the trailer now. They watched as the stocky Paint gelding lunged sideways and reared high on his hind legs. Lynn jumped out of the way just in time to avoid a flailing front hoof.

"That animal is going to hurt someone one of these days." Concern knitted Kari's brow.

"That's what John said."

Kari eyed her sister. "When did he say that?"

Pam shrugged her shoulders. "At the last show, I think. He saw those two guys trying to help Lynn load that monster." Pam giggled. "He also said, he would shoot the stupid thing, if it belonged to him. Of course, I don't think he really meant it."

Kari shook her head. "No, but at least he would train him to load properly."

Kari led Poco to the other side of the Williams' barn and tethered him. She looked around at her sister. "I wish I could afford to rent a trailer on my own. Maybe next year, when your little mare is old enough to show."

Lynn turned on them angrily when the girls walked up to the trailer. "It's about time. I could use some help."

Kari picked up the rope Lynn had coiled by the trailer. "I thought we were going to try it with Poco loading first."

"I changed my mind," Lynn snapped. She yanked angrily on Chief's halter, circling him away from the trailer. "Besides, that stupid horse of yours is so head-shy, he would probably go crazy if Chief so much as bumped him getting in."

Kari studied her friend. She couldn't believe what she was hearing. "What's bothering you?"

"Nothing," Lynn snapped.

"Something must be. What you said about Poco isn't true, and you know it." Kari studied her friend's back when Lynn turned her attention back to her horse. "Did I do something?"

Lynn didn't answer.

Kari threaded a rope through one of the metal rings at the back of the trailer. Letting the end dangle free, she walked around the ramp to the other side. Once the other end was threaded through a ring, Kari motioned for Pam to pick up the loose end.

Kari laid the rope on the ground in a half circle behind the trailer ramp. "Okay, bring him on up."

Lynn led Chief to the ramp. He walked stiff-legged until he reached the wooden incline. There he stopped, planted all four feet, and refused to budge. Lynn swung his head back and forth to get him off balance, but the horse stood firm.

Kari and Pam slowly pulled the rope through the rings until it rested gently behind Chief's buttocks.

Kari nodded to Lynn. She pulled on Chief's halter. As she pulled, Kari and Pam tightened the pressure on the rope. Chief lifted a front hoof and pawed at the wooden ramp. Slowly, he put his weight down as Kari pulled the rope tighter. The horse edged forward and lifted his other foreleg. As his weight hit the ramp, it creaked loudly. Chief bolted, pulling the leather lead from Lynn's hands. The big Paint sat back on his haunches and flipped backwards over the rope. Pam released her end as the horse's full weight hit the rope. Kari's end snaked through her hand before she could let go. She winced and clutched her rope-burned hand. Through tears of pain, she could see Lynn's shocked face.

"I'm okay," she assured her. "Get that beast back up here."

Pam stood on the other side of the ramp, a stunned look on her face. Slowly, she bent to retrieve her end of the rope as Lynn led Chief back to the ramp.

Lynn turned tear-filled eyes to Kari. "Maybe we should cancel showing today."

Mr. Williams came out of the barn carrying a bucket of oats. "Nonsense," he yelled, overhearing Lynn's comment. "Here, let's try this." He handed the bucket to Kari and picked up her end of the rope.

"But, Dad," Lynn protested. "Kari . . ."

Kari waved her off as she quickly climbed into the trailer to hide her pain.

If either set of parents knew one of the girls had gotten injured, they would probably put an end to the horse showing.

Pam and Mr. Williams tightened the rope as Chief approached the ramp. Kari swished the oats around in the bucket. The horse's ears pricked forward at the sound. He placed first one and then the other foot on the ramp. The pressure on the rope increased. The horse resisted, gathered himself, and lunged over the ramp. The force of the horse's lunge rocked the trailer. Kari braced herself to keep from falling.

Mr. Williams fastened the woven strap across the opening to keep Chief from backing out. Kari grabbed the dangling lead and tied up his head. The horse continued to dance nervously.

"Run, get Poco," said Mr. Williams.

Kari climbed from the trailer. Pam had already gone after Poco and was leading him back around the barn. She looked at her sister's hand with concern when Kari reached for Poco's lead.

"It's fine," Kari reassured her. She took the strap from Pam and led him to the ramp. The horse had always been an easy loader and Kari didn't expect any trouble. He lowered his head and sniffed at the rotting wood.

Chief continued his tantrum, stomping his feet and snorting.

Kari urged Poco into the trailer. He placed one foot gingerly on the wood, then the other, and started up the ramp.

Chief tried to back out. He leaned heavily on the aging strap across his buttocks. Kari hoped it would hold. It didn't. As Chief jumped backward, the fraying strap snapped like a firecracker. Kari ducked as the heavy woven fabric shot outward and whipped across Poco's face. His pupils rolled back, showing the whites of his eyes, and his ears were plastered flat to his head. He reared back on his hind legs, then dropped. His front legs hit the ramp with a force the rotting wood couldn't withstand. There was a sickening sound as the wood splintered and Poco's foreleg went through the ramp. Kari watched in horror as the wood gave way and her horse fell. He fought to free himself by sliding his other foreleg up under him.

"Quick," screamed Kari, "throw me the rope." She pushed it under his belly and threw the ends to Mr. Williams. He looped them through the rings on the trailer.

"Pam," she yelled, "get over here and help me pull."

Using the looped rope like a pulley, the four of them freed the big gelding.

He sank to the grass and lay deathly still. Kari knelt beside him stroking his sweating neck. She sat in a daze while blood oozed from the wound on his upper leg.

"Should I call Dr. Ackers?" Pam asked.

Kari stared at her sister for one confused moment and then went into action. "I'll do it," she said jumping to her feet. She grabbed a clean rag from the tack box and placed it over the wound. "Keep some pressure on this."

Kari took off at a dead run. Mr. Williams had already dialed the number by the time Kari reached the back door. Her hands were shaking as she took the phone receiver from his hands. She held it to her ear and waited for an answer. Five, six, seven rings.

"Please let someone be there," Kari prayed.

"High Street Clinic." John's voice came over the wire.

Kari was sobbing. "Oh, John, please help—it's Poco—he fell through a ramp."

"Kari, listen to me." John said urgently. "Is he up or down?"

"Down."

"Any bleeding?"

"Yes." Kari's voice wavered. "Above the knee. It's a pretty big gash."

"Okay, you know what to do." John's voice sounded calm and reassuring on the other end of the line. "Keep him down, if possible, and press a clean cloth over the wound. We'll be right there."

It was only a fifteen-minute drive from the clinic, but to Kari it seemed like hours before she saw Dr. Ackers's familiar black Blazer pull in the Williams's driveway.

John jumped out of the truck and hurried over to examine Poco. Dr. Ackers followed, carrying his large black medical bag. He crouched beside John and tenderly prodded both forelegs.

"Have you tried to get him up?" he asked.

Kari shook her head.

The veterinarian looked at John. "Let's have a go at it. Take the other side."

They rolled Poco over onto his other side. The vet stood up. "Now let's see if he can get that good leg under him."

The big horse grunted and scrambled to his feet. He balanced on three legs and let his injured leg dangle.

Kari held Poco's lead while Dr. Ackers carefully examined the leg.

"It doesn't look like anything is broken, but he may have sprained a tendon." The veterinarian turned to John. "I'm going to have to put a couple of sutures in the leg, but let's try to get him home first."

The short walk across the backyard was a tedious one. Poco hobbled along on three legs, his fourth leg sporting a temporary bandage.

As they reached the barn Tim arrived. Kari noticed his bright red sports car pull into the driveway. She glanced at Pam. "What's he doing here?"

Her sister shrugged.

"Tell him I'll be there in a minute," called Kari. "Fill him in on what happened."

Pam crossed her arms in disgust. "I don't think I'll have to."

Kari turned back toward the house. She couldn't hear what was being said, but Lynn was talking to Tim, her arms moving in wild animation. He reached over and placed a comforting arm around her shoulders.

Kari turned back to the barn where Dr. Ackers had started to work on Poco. John stood close by, ready to hand the veterinarian the needed supplies. Dr. Ackers cleaned the wound carefully and readied the sutures. He looked briefly at Kari. "There's no muscle damage and the stitches ought to heal in no time."

John smiled his encouragement before he bent over the vet's shoulder to watch him insert the stitches.

After Poco's leg had been sewn up, Dr. Ackers stepped out of the stall and handed Kari a roll of bandages. "Why don't you help him finish up, Kari. I'll go talk to your mom and dad."

Kari took the bandages and stepped into the stall. She had wrapped many horses' legs since she had started to work at the clinic, but never after they had had surgery. She looked down at Poco's leg and noticed Dr. Ackers had already applied the dressing and first layer of gauze.

John reached for the roll of sterile wrapping. As Kari laid the roll of bandages in his outstretched hand, their fingers touched. Again, the brief encounter sent shock waves through her body. She yanked her hand back as though her fingers had been burned by a flame. John didn't seem to notice as he secured the bandages on Poco's leg.

He was just finishing when Tim burst into the barn.

His gaze roamed over John, then Poco, and then came to rest on Kari. "Well, he finally did it, didn't he? That stupid, crazy horse of yours. Someone could have gotten hurt."

"Someone did," Kari shot at him.

Tim's face turned red with anger. "I'm not talking about that worthless animal."

Kari held up her injured hand. "Neither am I," she said softly. "Only Poco wasn't responsible for this, Chief was."

Tim stared at her hand for a moment. "Is it bad?"

"I think I'll survive."

John turned his back on Tim to quiet Poco who was becoming nervous from all the yelling. He shook his head and snorted.

Tim looked at the horse. His anger returned. "So now you want to blame Lynn for all of this. Do you have any idea how upset your friend is right now? Do you even care?"

Tim stormed out of the barn. Kari was miserable. She felt sick to her stomach and her head was spinning. Everything was a mess. Was she to blame?

She sank to her knees in the clean bed of straw. The tears

she had been holding back filled her eyes and spilled down her cheeks. John touched her shoulder lightly as he crouched beside her.

"Things will work out," he said softly.

Kari shook her head and the tears flowed faster.

"But you were right." Kari's voice was strained. "He went crazy when that strap flew up in his face. This never would have happened if he . . ."

"You can't blame yourself." John gently took her hand and turned it palm up. "That's a nasty rope burn." He tore open a sterile gauze pad, placed it over the burn.

Kari sniffed as she watched Poco take a couple of tentative steps on his injured leg. He was his normal docile self again.

"Why do people do things like that?"

"Like what?" John questioned. He lightly wrapped tape around the gauze pad.

"Why do they mistreat animals?"

John let out a weary sigh. He leaned back against the support pole and slid to a sitting position. "I don't know. We get horses at the clinic every day that have been abused or used carelessly. It can turn them into crazy animals."

Kari looked at him in despair. "But Poco isn't crazy. He would never hurt me on purpose. No matter what anyone thinks."

She sat down in the straw and pulled her knees up under her chin. "Oh, John, what am I going to do now?"

John put an arm around Kari's shoulders and gently pulled her against him. She rested her head on his shoulder and closed her eyes. She felt protected in John's arms, and she moved closer. She wanted to tell him the problem wasn't just Poco. She needed him to understand. Her whole world was so mixed-up. Everything was whirling around in her brain until she thought it would explode. It wasn't just Poco. It was her relationship with Lynn, and her breakup with Tim—everything. But most of all, it was her feelings for John. They were new and confusing, totally beyond her experience. How could she explain to John how she felt? She couldn't even explain it to herself.

It was as though John sensed her turmoil. He cradled her in his arms and some of the despair eased.

Kari could hear his heartbeat where her head rested against his chest. His warm breath sent little shivers down her spine. The closeness to John was intoxicating. Kari could smell the spicy scent of his after-shave mixed with the antiseptic smell of the clinic. She timidly raised her head to examine his face. It was expressionless except for his eyes. They had turned a dark, smoky blue and Kari felt his heartbeat quicken. Her own heartbeat quickened in response. She raised her hand to touch his cheek. John's dark lashes closed over his eyes and he lowered his head to meet Kari's. His lips feathered kisses on her eyelids, her cheek, and then found her mouth. At first the touch of his lips was light, uncertain. He pulled back and looked down at her.

There was a spark of some indefinable emotion in his eyes. "Kari, I . . ." he hesitated, his voice thick with emotion.

Kari lifted her mouth in silent invitation. His kiss was warm and gentle and totally consumed her consciousness. She pressed her body tighter to his, her blood raced. John pulled her even closer.

Then he reluctantly drew back, his breathing uneven. Clasping both of Kari's hands in his own, he pulled them from around his neck. He knelt in front of her and stared at her for a long moment.

John's voice broke the silence. "I'd better go. . . . Dr. Ackers is waiting."

He stood up, pulling Kari with him. His eyes brimmed with tenderness as he gazed into her own. "Are you okay now?"

Kari nodded ever so slightly, still caught up in the magical spell of his embrace. Standing on tiptoe, she touched her lips timidly to his.

He crushed her against him in a brief bearlike hug before bending to retrieve the medical bag. He paused at the barn door and looked back at Kari. A brief smile touched his lips. Then he was gone.

Kari watched his retreating back. She couldn't deny the spark of excitement his kisses had created. She raised a finger to her lips, still tingling from his touch.

"Good-bye, John," she whispered. "I love you."

10

KARI WAS singing when she walked into the clinic the next morning. Donna looked up and smiled. "That's a good sign. Everything is all right with your horse?"

Kari walked over and stashed her purse in the desk. "He had to have several stitches so I can't ride him for a while, but he'll be fine in a couple of weeks."

Donna finished writing in a folder and handed it to Kari to file. "John was telling me about what happened when he came in this morning."

Kari's heart skipped, and she hid a smile from Donna. "Oh, is John working in the clinic today?" She hoped her voice sounded normal, because she didn't feel normal at all. She felt light, giddy, and carefree. Since John had been working with the field veterinarians, she rarely saw him.

All morning Kari looked for excuses to run to the back of the clinic, but Donna kept her busy answering the telephone and making appointments. She glanced at her watch every five minutes, willing the noon hour to arrive. When the hands on the large office clock read twelve, Kari announced she was going to lunch.

"Good," said Donna, "I'm tired of hard-boiled eggs. Do you want to get pizza or burgers?"

Kari took a long time freshening her lip gloss. She was hoping to have lunch with John, but she didn't want to hurt Donna's feelings.

The hesitation didn't go unnoticed. Donna looked at Kari and smiled wisely. "You don't have to hit me with a brick. Were you planning on having lunch with John?"

Kari knew she hadn't been hiding her feelings very well. She blushed slightly. "I was hoping to, but he hasn't asked."

Donna folded her arms across her chest. "I don't believe what I'm hearing. Isn't this the day of women's lib? Besides, that's a serious one, that John Garrett. He might take a little chasing."

"Serious?" Kari shook her head. "Not with his sense of humor."

Donna smiled. "Oh, you'd be surprised at the insecurities jokes and flirting can cover." She gave Kari a little shove. "Now march right back there and ask him to go with you."

Bolstered by Donna's pep talk, Kari walked determinedly through the swinging door.

John was walking up the hall in her direction. She couldn't help but notice how his jeans molded to his lean hips and the cotton of his shirt strained across his broad shoulders. She paused and waited for his long, swinging strides to bring him to her.

When he stopped in front of her and rested one hand against the wall without smiling, Kari nearly lost her nerve.

She cleared her throat. "Are you eating lunch today?"

"Not today." His gaze darted quickly from her face to the wall to the ceiling and finally came to focus on an area of the floor just in front of his toe.

His uneasiness didn't escape Kari's scrutiny. Could John possibly be as unsure as she was herself? A pinkish tinge touched his tanned cheeks. Was John actually blushing?

A smile parted Kari's lips as she examined the handsome planes of his face. How she loved him at that moment. Maybe even more than she had before. Now he seemed more real, as vulnerable as she was, and maybe even attainable.

The awkward moment ended when Dr. Ackers walked out of the nearby recovery room. He glanced at the two of them. "We're almost ready, John. You'd better get into a sterile gown."

John nodded to Dr. Ackers. Turning his attention back to Kari, he explained. "Dr. Ackers is doing some pretty complicated leg surgery. He's allowing me to observe." His eyes met hers briefly before he walked away.

She didn't see John again until late the next afternoon when she wandered back to the stall area of the clinic. The clinic was a large, modern facility with thirty regular stalls and two isolation stalls for the horses. Kari glanced around at the immaculate surroundings. Several afternoons a week, she walked back to check on the different patients. Each one received specialized care and treatment, and although she had nothing to do with their immediate care, she had run tests on many of them. She knew them all by name and knew their medical histories from their files.

Kari looked through the slatted upper portion of a stall and a sleek bay Saddlebred turned his head to look at her. It was the young stallion who had had leg surgery the day before. It was not uncommon for the veterinarians to have to perform surgery on a horse's legs. Indeed, it seemed to Kari that the delicate leg bones caused as much trouble as all the other ailments put together. But this horse's surgery had been extremely serious. The valuable show stallion had broken his leg while at a show in the area. There were several fractures in the bones close to his foot and a heavy plaster cast had to be applied to his hind leg. Kari was reminded how lucky she was that Poco only had to have stitches.

"Will he be all right?" Kari asked as John came to stand by her.

He rested his hands against the slatted portion of the stall and watched the bay stallion hobble around the sawdust-covered interior. "He should be, in time. Of course, he will never be able to show again."

Kari watched the sleek animal for several seconds. "That's too bad; he's so beautiful."

John nodded his agreement. "He was already quite successful in the show ring, so they will probably use him for stud."

John turned his back and leaned against the stall so he was facing Kari. He stared at her for a long moment before speaking. "Dr. Ackers thought one of us should check Poco's leg this evening. I told him I would take care of it." John looked down at his feet. He dug at the clay floor with the toe of his boot. "All right if I stop by when I'm finished here?"

Kari studied his profile for a minute before answering. The idea of getting to spend a few more minutes with him was a nice surprise. "Yes, of course, it's all right."

John pushed himself away from the stall. "Then I'll see you later this evening."

As soon as Kari arrived home, she ran to her room to fix her hair, freshen her lip gloss, and spray on just a touch of perfume. She gave Pam strict orders not to follow her to the barn. "This is one time I don't want your company," she teased.

Pam giggled. "Can't I even watch from the hayloft?"

"Watch what?" Kari demanded.

"In case he kisses you again." Pam ducked out of Kari's reach as she whirled around. "I mean, how am I ever going to learn?"

Kari blushed bright red. "Pam Stewart, you sneak." She tossed a pillow at her sister. "Where were you?"

The devil danced in Pam's eyes. "I went back down to the barn while Dr. Ackers was talking to Mom and Dad, but I noticed you didn't need any help."

Kari covered her mouth with her hand. "Oh, no! You didn't say anything to Mom or Dad, did you?"

Pam looked irritated. "I'm no blabbermouth." She followed Kari down the steps and out the back door. "Do you think he will ask you out?"

"I'm not sure. At first he was really friendly and teased me a lot." Kari sat down on the back porch where she could watch the driveway. "But the last couple of days he's acted really strange. I don't know. Maybe he's sorry he kissed me." She looked helplessly at her sister. "Maybe it didn't mean anything to him and he doesn't know how to tell me and he's afraid I'll get the wrong idea and, oh, I don't know." Kari paused and gasped for breath.

Pam looked pensive. "Or maybe he really likes you and is too shy to say so."

"I don't think so." Then Kari remembered her conversation with Donna and how John had behaved in the hall outside the recovery room. She'd thought at the time that he'd seemed very reserved, almost shy.

The conversation ended when John's red and gray Chevy pickup pulled into the driveway. Pam gave her a thumbs up sign as she left the porch.

Kari caught up with John halfway to the barn. She was running to match his fast pace. He noticed her jogging steps and shortened his stride to fall into step beside her. Kari looked up at him. "Do you always run?"

John laughed. It was the same lighthearted sound as on the first night she had met him. It touched Kari's heart and made her happy. Maybe she was just imagining his moods.

When they entered the barn, Poco was standing in his stall pulling wisps of hay from the manger. John knelt down beside him and Kari held his halter.

She watched John's hands, long-fingered and strong, as he removed the bandages. The wound was healing nicely and very little swelling remained. John ran his fingers up and down the leg to check for any further complications. Poco seemed fine.

John stood up and slapped the sorrel's thick neck. "He'll be good as new in a few days, but I'd take it a little easy on that leg for a while."

"How long?" Kari asked.

John scratched his head. "Well, you should start walking him around now. You can put some weight on his back in a few more days." He paused and rested his hands on his hips. "As for showing, I think you'd better give him a couple of weeks."

"What you really think is that I should never put him in the show ring." Kari countered.

John let out a long, exasperated sigh. "That's not exactly what I said."

"You said he would never make a show horse."

"What I said was, he would never make a show horse unless you could overcome his head-shyness." John backed her against the stall door and grinned down at her. "You have very selective hearing, my dear."

Kari thrust her chin out stubbornly. "Okay, if you're such an expert, show me how to train him."

His eyes danced with mischief as he returned her stare. "I'd be happy to. It's only one of my many talents."

Kari laughed and playfully shoved him out of the way. He caught her arm and gently drew her to him. The laughter caught in her throat as Kari tilted her head to look him full in the face.

He entwined his fingers together at the back of her waist and pulled her closer. "Dr. Ackers didn't really send me out here," he confessed.

"He didn't?"

John shook his head and a mischievous smile played across his lips. "Doc told your dad he could take the bandages off himself."

Her knees felt like the center of a jelly doughnut, and she braced her hands against the hard wall of his chest for balance as his arms tightened. He's going to kiss me, she thought, as she leaned forward slightly.

Just then, Mr. Stewart called from outside the barn.

John released her and turned away abruptly.

"In here, Dad," answered Kari, hoping her voice would give nothing away.

Mr. Stewart came into the barn. "How's this big red horse doing?"

The question was directed at John, but Kari answered. "John says he's doing fine."

"So this is John," he said, extending his hand. "Dr. Ackers told me a lot about this young man, but I didn't get a chance to meet him the other day."

"Then I'll introduce you," Kari said, throwing an exaggerated smile at her father. "Dad, I'd like you to meet John Garrett." She turned to John. "John, this is my father, Mr. Stewart."

John smiled briefly at her before he shook her father's hand.

Her father held onto John's hand and slapped him on the shoulder. "It's almost dinnertime, John. Why don't you stay and have a bite with us? Kari's mother makes a great roast."

Kari couldn't believe her ears. Her father was inviting John to dinner. Did he suspect how she felt about him? Kari held her breath, hoping John would say yes.

John looked first at Kari and then at her father. "I'm sorry, sir, but I can't, tonight."

"Some other time, then." Her father raised a hand in farewell and strode across the backyard.

Kari reached up and flipped off the barn lights. She lifted her face to the sky, breathing in the fresh evening air that brought a pleasant coolness to the hot June day. Her hand brushed against John's and her fingers tingled. She wondered if he felt it, too. She tried to imagine what it would be like to hold his hand as they walked. Reaching out her fingers tentatively, she touched his. They were warm and callused as she laced them with hers. The walk to the driveway was the shortest Kari could ever remember.

John released her hand when they reached the asphalt. He lowered the tailgate of his truck and sat down. "Kari, I've been thinking. Since you insist you want to show Poco, I think it's time for some concentrated effort."

Kari took up a seat on the tailgate alongside John. "But I work him every night."

"I'm aware of that, but I think he needs some specialized training."

Kari was puzzled. "What kind of specialized training?"

"Back to square one." John leaned against the side of the

truck and draped his arm over one propped-up knee. "I think we need to take Poco and start him from the very beginning— retrain him completely."

"I don't know anything about training a horse from scratch," Kari said.

John's laugh was a deep chuckle in his throat. "Don't panic, I said *we,*" John laughed. "I'll be happy to help if you want me to."

Kari considered the proposition and decided it had definite possibilities. Besides curing Poco's head problem, she would be spending a lot more time with John. She was careful to keep her voice calm. "Well, if you really don't mind helping, I sure could use your expertise."

"I'm off tomorrow and so are you," he reminded her. "We could give it a try in the afternoon."

Kari spoke with a calm she did not feel. "Sounds fine to me." She couldn't believe how things were turning out. It was like one of her daydreams coming true.

She didn't think anything could spoil her fantasy of that moment until she heard the roar of the little sports car engine as it turned into the driveway. Kari drew in her breath sharply as Tim pulled up beside the truck and got out.

His gaze rested on John. "Seems like I've been running into you a lot lately. Did we have another emergency here or what?"

Kari's mouth dropped open in surprise. She was too stunned to speak.

John stood up stiffly and motioned Kari to do the same. He slammed the tailgate shut and climbed into the truck. His eyes were cold and aloof as he glared down at Tim. "Don't worry, I was just checking the stitches in the horse's leg." He gunned the truck's motor and sped out of the driveway.

"That was uncalled for, Tim," Kari said, furious. "He was just here doing his job." It depressed Kari to think that might be the only reason he was there.

Tim swaggered over to Kari. "Is he the reason you dumped me?"

"One has nothing to do with the other."

"Oh, really?" Tim smirked and his eyes narrowed nastily. "You're so hung up on that dumb cowboy, you can't think straight."

Kari was infuriated to hear John referred to as a dumb cowboy. "I'm not hung up on him," she said. "He is just someone I work with at the clinic. And another thing, he is not a dumb cowboy. He is studying to be an equine veterinarian."

"That's just perfect." Tim started laughing. "You can mess up the horses, and he can stitch them back together."

Kari had never hit anyone in her whole life, but her fingers itched to slap Tim. She turned on her heel and stalked away before she did something foolish.

Tim came after her and grabbed her arm.

Kari pulled away. "We're through, Tim. Finished! I tried to tell you that the other night. Will you please leave?"

Tim reached out for her hand, but she pulled it away. "Look, Kari, I'm sorry. I didn't mean those things I just said, and I didn't come here to argue with you."

She glared at him. "Then why did you come? It seems every time we're together we argue. I can't take any more."

Tim sighed and his voice softened. "I know. I said I was sorry." Kari watched him as he nervously fiddled with his keys. "I really like you, Kari. I thought maybe we could try again."

Kari shook her head sadly. "I don't think so, Tim."

He shrugged his thin shoulders and turned back to his car. "If you'd rather tramp around in a filthy barn instead of going to an exclusive country club, that's your business."

Tim lowered his tall frame into the Fiat and looked back at Kari. "You'll never get anywhere with a bum like that." The little engine roared to life and Tim yelled over the din, "Don't say I didn't warn you, Kari."

She watched the taillights as he pulled out of the driveway. She knew breaking up with Tim had been for the best. Even if her relationship with John went no further, she knew she couldn't have continued dating him. She was glad she was mature enough to stand on her own two feet.

𝒔 *11* 𝒔

THE NEXT morning was gray and overcast. Kari looked out the window and frowned. "Please don't rain," she pleaded to the sky. This day had to be perfect; she had it all planned. She would wear her best jeans, her new boots and her favorite green blouse. It was going to be a wonderful afternoon, she just knew it.

Slipping on shorts and a T-shirt, she quickly made her bed and went down the hall to get the cleaning supplies from the linen closet.

Kari's thoughts returned to the evening before and John's playful teasing. She hoped he would be like that today. When he was quiet and serious, she didn't know what to say to him.

Kari tried to push the thoughts of John to the back of her mind. The morning was going to be long enough without thinking of him constantly.

She put extra energy into cleaning the bathroom and sweeping the upstairs hall. When she started on the downstairs with the same vigor, her mother looked at her suspiciously. "I thought you would sleep late this morning. Mind you, I'm not complaining, but I usually have trouble getting you to make your bed."

Kari made a face at her mother. "I'll go sunbathe, if you'd prefer." She gathered up the dirty towels and carried them to the basement.

After she finished the downstairs bath and vacuumed the living room, she went to the kitchen to check on the time. The clock read only nine-thirty. Kari groaned. The morning was going to last forever.

She slipped on her tennis shoes and headed to the barn. Poco's stall had to be cleaned and that would keep her busy for a while.

She tied Poco outside his stall. He reached through the

111

slatted boards and picked at some hay while Kari got the pitch-fork. She went to work mucking out his stall and putting in clean bedding. It was hard work, but Kari didn't mind. She enjoyed working around the horses. She decided she liked that better than anything else. It's what made her job at the clinic so perfect. She felt she was really accomplishing something.

Kari finished the barn work and still had plenty of time to spare. She decided she would call the specialty shop and check on the awards. It hadn't been that long since she ordered them, but she thought she would check anyway.

When she gave her report to the Ohio Junior Riders' meeting last week, she had been able to say that the awards had been ordered, exactly what was ordered, and how much they were going to cost. What she didn't know was whether she had made the right choices and how they would look. Kari hoped every-thing would work out.

She dialed the telephone and waited for the answer on the other end.

"Hello, this is Kari Stewart from the Ohio Junior Riders. I wanted to check on the status of the awards I ordered."

There was a good-natured laugh at the end of the line. "Rather anxious about those awards, aren't you, young lady? The good news from the company is that everything is on schedule, and they will be shipped in plenty of time for your show."

Kari thanked the man for his patience and hung up. She didn't want to be a nuisance, but the awards were her first big project, and she wanted to make sure everything came off without a hitch.

She glanced at the kitchen clock one more time before going upstairs to change.

John arrived a little after noon. He nodded to her as he got out of his truck and walked by the back porch. Kari figured he would stop and wait for her. When he continued to walk to the barn, she jumped up and hurried to catch up with him.

"You're running again," she teased. John threw her a side-ways glance, but didn't smile. Kari had a terrible feeling that he was going to be in one of his quiet moods. She wondered what was wrong.

John paused at the opening of the barn and looked at her sharply. "I wasn't sure you still wanted me to show up today."

Kari was annoyed by his curt tone. "I told you I did." She brushed by John and continued into the barn. She heard his sharp intake of breath as her shoulder collided with his arm. Kari didn't know why he was angry. She certainly hadn't done anything.

Once inside the barn, Kari headed for the tack room. She pulled the lunge rope from a hook and fastened it to Poco's halter.

The sorrel gelding seemed to enjoy being let out of his stall. Ever since Kari had bought him, he had been allowed to run in the pasture. He didn't like being confined in the barn. He limped eagerly beside her as she led him to the fenced ring.

"Poor boy," she soothed, patting his shining red neck. "It's only for a few more days until your stitches come out."

John laughed softly and some of the tension eased in Kari. She hadn't heard his boots approach in the soft surface of the ring and was startled when his voice sounded right beside her.

"Do you think he understands what you're saying?"

"Probably not, but at least I got you to laugh," she said softly. "Why were you angry with me?"

John turned and looked down at her with eyes that held a painful and faraway look. His sigh was audible and weary. "I wasn't angry with you."

Kari was confused. "Then what?"

A disgusted look crossed John's face. "I was angry with myself."

"But why?"

"It doesn't matter," he answered. "I'm sorry if I was rude."

Kari didn't want his apology. She just wanted things to be light and open between them again.

Putting Poco on the rail, Kari started him around the ring at a slow walk.

John stood behind her and observed Poco with a critical eye as he gave her directions. "Okay, move him out a little . . . now stop him . . . have him reverse."

John nodded approvingly. "You have him working pretty smoothly on the line. I think we'll start setting his head." He crouched by the horse's front legs and took a quick look at the healing wound. "Looks pretty good. Go ahead and tack him up."

Kari led Poco to the end of the ring where John had set the saddle. She watched with interest while he slipped an unusual-looking apparatus over Poco's head. It was comprised of several leather straps. One draped over the horse's withers, another fastened to the saddle cinch, while two shorter ones extended out from the chest and allowed the reins to pass through.

"It's called a running martingale," he explained to Kari's wide-eyed look. "It allows some play in the head, but prevents him from sticking his nose in the air like he usually does."

John demonstrated how the martingale worked. "This is just for training, you understand, they won't allow it in a Western Pleasure class."

He stood on the left side of the horse away from the rail and motioned to Kari. "Come here." His strong fingers clasped her arm and pulled her over in front of him. He reached his muscular arms around her and grasped each of her hands in one of his. Kari was glad he was standing behind her so he could not see her blush. He placed a hand on each rein and positioned one on each side of the horse's neck a little higher than the withers.

Kari laughed nervously. "It's a good thing Poco isn't any bigger, otherwise, I would have to do this on stilts."

John released her hands and backed away. "Since he's pretty well neck-reined, he'll probably do this exercise without some-one leading him." John waved his arm in a signal for Kari to start Poco around the ring.

They worked for almost half an hour before John called the session to a halt. "You only need to work him for about twenty minutes or he'll get bored with the routine. Run him through it twice a day, working him from both sides."

"How long should I do it?" Kari questioned.

"For about a week, then we'll work him with you on his back."

Kari led Poco to the barn, fastened him in a cross-tie and pulled the saddle from his back.

John followed her into the barn carrying some balloons, plastic flags, and an umbrella.

"Are we going to have some kind of weird party?" Kari asked laughingly as she eyed the odd paraphernalia.

John's response was an exaggerated wink. "Poco gets to have the party." He blew up several balloons and tied them around a support post near the sorrel horse. Poco's head flew up as the balloons bounced and swayed. Picking up a brush, John began grooming the horse, talking to him in a soft, soothing voice the entire time. Soon Poco's ears relaxed and he lowered his head.

Kari watched the whole process. "Will this cure his head-shyness?"

"Let's hope so." John untied the balloons and slowly moved them toward the horse's head. He bounced them gently against Poco's cheek before he handed them to Kari.

"Since your horse has probably been beaten, you'll have to totally rebuild his trust in humans." John turned Poco loose in his stall. "Once he realizes that things flying around his head aren't going to hurt him, he won't be as apt to shy."

John gathered up the saddle, flags, and brightly colored umbrella and carried them to the tack room. He placed the saddle on its stand and picked up a book Kari had left sitting on the shelf.

"Reading up, huh?" He waved the book at her as she followed him into the room.

Kari noticed he had picked up one of her books on veterinary medicine. She wondered if she should tell him the truth.

"Looks like my deep, dark secret is out," she joked.

He looked up from the book he was scanning. "It does have a way of getting in your blood, doesn't it?"

Kari nodded. "Only I'm afraid I was hooked long before I started working at the clinic." She started giggling. "Do you know, I used to pretend our dog was my patient and I would practice putting splints on his legs and bandaging him."

"You, too?" John joined in her laughter. "I suppose you took in all the stray cats as well."

"And nursed baby birds that fell out of their nests."

"I even raised a pair of baby raccoons when their mother was killed on the road."

"I've gone you one better," teased Kari. "Once I brought home a nest of baby field mice from camp in my Kleenex box. They were so little, they didn't even have their eyes open. Would you believe I tried to keep them alive by feeding them with an eyedropper?"

They laughed openly, freely, before John's face became serious again. "I guess we share the same obsession."

Kari felt very close to him at that moment. She had shared her hopes, her innermost dreams with him, and he hadn't laughed or told her she was crazy. He understood.

They stood staring at each other for several seconds before

John broke the silence. "Mind if I borrow this?" He held up the book.

Kari shook her head and smiled. "Help yourself."

"I'll give it back to you at the clinic or the next time I come out."

Kari said good-bye to him at the truck and made plans for the next training session.

On the following Wednesday, John stopped by for Poco's second lesson.

"The first thing we're going to do is string some flags," he said, striding towards the barn.

Kari jogged alongside. "Why the flags?" she panted.

John came to an abrupt stop. He looked down at her and laughed. "I'm running again, aren't I?" He reached over and grasped Kari's hand. "I'll try to remember to slow down."

Kari got goose bumps at his touch. She entwined her fingers with his as they walked.

"Why are you using the flags?" she asked again as they reached the tack room.

John pulled the string of triangular flags out of the box. "Because they're bright and make a lot of noise when they flap in the wind—two things that are liable to set a horse off right away."

He climbed up one side of the slatted stall and fastened one end of the string of flags in the corner. Running them along the front of the open box stall, he secured the other end. "There," he said, stepping back to admire his handiwork. "That will keep them out of his reach, but they'll still be visible."

Kari watched the bright plastic flags move ever so slightly in the hot June air. "Looks a little like a gas station grand opening," she mused.

John pretended to scowl at her before he turned to lead Poco from the other stall. The sorrel's head flew up when he saw the brightly colored flags. He pranced sideways as John led him to a far corner of the barn. John tacked him up and Kari hoisted herself into the saddle.

"Keep him to a walk," John cautioned her. "We don't want to put too much stress on that leg."

Kari moved him slowly to the ring while John walked along beside her. Once inside, she put Poco on the rail and John took a position in the center of the ring. At first Poco was reluctant to obey the commands Kari was giving him, and John was forced to walk along at his shoulder to reinforce the signals. But after a few times around the ring Poco was taking the commands and working smoothly.

"Much better," called John. "I think he's going to be a star pupil."

Kari pulled the stocky gelding to a halt and patted his neck lovingly. "I knew he would be."

John grabbed Poco's bridle and smiled up at her. "He still has a long way to go, but at least he's not fighting us." Poco turned his head and John rubbed the side of his cheek affectionately. "Well, big fella, I think you've had enough for today." Looking up at Kari, he added, "We don't want to overdo it and have him turn sour on us."

Kari agreed as she turned Poco toward the barn.

The next couple of weeks flew by. When Kari wasn't working at the clinic, she was busy with Poco. She worked him twice a day and carefully followed John's instructions.

Slowly but surely, the sorrel horse began to respond. Kari couldn't be sure who was happier with the progress, she or John.

Although he had not tried to kiss her again, she felt very close to him. They often worked in a companionable silence or discussed their future plans at great length.

Kari decided if her relationship with him developed no further than the special friendship they shared, she still had experienced something very worthwhile.

But that didn't stop her from dreaming about him, or from loving him.

12

It HAD been over four weeks since Poco's accident. The June bills had all been mailed out, and Donna didn't need Kari's help in the office.

"I'm going back to the lab then," she announced.

"I may join you," Donna joked. "Things are really slow up front this morning."

Kari made her way to the lab. First, she scrubbed and sterilized the instruments that had been used in surgery, then she checked her lab sheet to see what tests had to be made. Kari noted only two stool samples were scheduled. She got the specimens and took a seat at the lab table. She carefully made note of any sign of worms and recorded it on the individual charts.

Shortly before noon, she took a short break and walked back to the stalls to check on the young show stallion. He seemed glad to see her and hobbled over to the door to have his nose patted. She talked to him in soft, loving tones as she rubbed the velvety softness.

"If I put a cast on my leg, will you talk to me that way?" John's amused voice sounded directly from behind her.

This time Kari vowed she wouldn't be put off by his teasing. "Do you want your ears scratched and your nose patted, too?"

At the sound of his deep chuckle, Kari whirled around, but her smart comment caught in her throat. Instead of his usual jeans and Western shirt, John was wearing a dark pin-striped suit. Kari thought he looked like a successful young businessman. She couldn't take her eyes off him; never had she seen him look so handsome.

The stallion pulled at her blouse, looking for more attention, but she was unaware of his tugging as she was caught and held by John's piercing blue stare.

"Looks like you've made another friend." Dr. Ackers's voice

118

boomed from behind John. Kari turned her head to smile at the older man.

"If you don't quit making such a fuss over all the patients, they're never going to want to leave." Dr. Ackers looked at John. "I think Kari is our resident love supply. All the horses, even the difficult ones, respond to her. I think we might have to keep her around permanently. How about it, young lady, are you interested?"

Kari's voice raced with excitement. "That would be great! Then I could work here while I'm studying to be a vet."

This time there was no surprise on Dr. Ackers's face. "You really are serious about this."

"You bet I am," she said.

The Doctor's glance slid from Kari to John. "So that's why you were picking up that literature at the university. By the way, have you told Kari the good news?"

"What good news?" Kari watched an embarrassed grin spread across John's face as he shuffled his feet uncomfortably. "Not yet."

"Not had the chance, huh?" Dr. Ackers draped an arm around each of their shoulders as they walked back to the main part of the clinic. "I'll leave you two to your errand. I've got patients to attend to." He directed his next question at John. "Since you're going into town, would you pick up that box of ointment from the medical supply?" Dr. Ackers left them and walked into one of the examining rooms.

Kari looked at John with a puzzled expression. "What errand? And Dr. Ackers said the two of us. Am I going someplace?"

"Yes," teased John. "I'm taking you away from all this."

"I don't want to be taken away from all this."

John tilted his head towards her. "Not even to pick up some trophies and ribbons?"

"They're in?" Kari cried. "I can hardly wait to see them! Let's go right now."

The ride into town was a quiet one. It wasn't a strained silence, but a comfortable one. Kari was content just to be with John and occasionally steal a glance at him while he was driving.

When they reached downtown Dayton, they went to the medical supply house first. It was a lot like a warehouse with a small office in front. Kari waited in the truck while John

disappeared into the brick building. He returned a few minutes
later carrying the box of medical supplies and stashed it behind
the seat of the pickup.

"That takes care of Dr. Ackers's errand," he said getting
back in the truck. He looked over at Kari. "Now, do you want
to eat first or get the trophies?"

"Get the trophies." Kari didn't care that John was amused
by her excitement. Handling the awards was a big challenge
for her.

After they picked them up, she looked at John as she helped
him load the trophies in the truck. "Wouldn't you love to win
one of these?" Kari ran her fingers over the cold, smooth surface
of the horse statues atop the trophies. "Of course, you probably
have so many already that it's no big thing to you."

John grinned as he took the box from Kari's arms and placed
it on the front seat. "No matter how many times you win, it's
still a thrill. When you get out there and your horse is working
right and you know you did the best you could—you never
get tired of that feeling."

Kari had never had the thrill of winning a first place, but
she knew what John was saying. Every time she won any
ribbon, she felt she had accomplished something.

With the trophies and ribbons securely loaded they went to
find a place to eat lunch. John turned into a little hot dog stand
and looked over at Kari. "They have the best foot-longs here.
I hope you like Coney Island dogs."

Kari assured him she did as he swung the pickup into a
parking spot.

For most of lunch, Kari let John direct the conversation.
They talked openly about the coming horse show and the horses
at the clinic. Everything was going so smoothly that Kari was
almost afraid to ask the question that had been on her mind
since they left the clinic. Finally, she took a deep breath and
asked, "What was Dr. Ackers talking about at the clinic?" At
first John pretended not to understand her question. He ran
long, tapered fingers absentmindedly around the rim of his root-
beer mug. An unreadable expression passed over his face before
he looked away. His voice was just audible as he said, "I've
been awarded a scholarship at the university for next fall."
There was a note of pride in his voice, but his eyes seemed
wary, as if waiting for Kari's reaction.

Kari reached across the table and grabbed his arm. "That's

wonderful. You definitely deserve it. I've never seen anyone work so hard for something they wanted."

He was looking at Kari with a guarded expression. "They don't award this particular scholarship just on merit; part of it is based on need."

"And who doesn't need in this day and age?" Kari smiled to herself as she thought of Tim. "Well, I can think of a few."

John nodded, as if he knew she was thinking of Tim. "Yes, so can I, but some of us have to do it the hard way."

Kari ignored the comment and continued: "My parents are hoping my grades are good enough to get at least a partial scholarship. I mean, my parents both have good jobs, but it really would make things easier."

John seemed to relax. "Yeah, my parents have had it pretty tough the last couple of years. I guess any help is appreciated, especially with my grand ideas and six years of school ahead."

Kari wanted to ask why things were tough, but she didn't want to pry.

The conversation drifted back to the horse show. "If it's all right with your parents," John was saying, "I'll bring the awards by the house after work. We can go through them and see if everything checks out."

"Sounds good," agreed Kari.

The afternoon at the clinic went by slowly. There weren't any tests to run, and Kari had already put away the box of medical supplies. She wandered into the office to see if Donna had anything for her to do. When she came up empty-handed, Kari decided to go home a little early. It would give her time to work Poco before John came by with the awards.

The Stewarts had just finished eating dinner when Kari heard John's truck in the driveway. She met him on the back porch and ushered him into the kitchen for dessert.

Her mother stopped cutting the apple pie and turned to smile a welcome at John. "Kari said you got some rather exciting news today."

John returned her mother's smile. "Well, I guess it is. I got a scholarship to the university."

Kari's parents seemed impressed. They talked for some length about the clinic and John's planned career. Kari figured it was a perfect time to mention her own plans for the future. To her surprise, they had no objections. In fact, they seemed pleased she had decided on an interest to pursue.

When they had finished dessert, Kari and John went out to the truck to get the awards. Pam followed along to help. She picked up the box of blue ribbons and looked at them longingly. "Wouldn't it be great to have these hanging all over your room?"

Kari brushed by her with a box of trophies. "I'd settle for one."

John came up behind her. "While you're dreaming—dream big. Settle for two, one in Horsemanship and one in Western Pleasure."

Kari looked up at him in surprise and the teasing tone left his voice. "You could, you're good enough, and now that Poco is starting to work more like a pleasure horse and less like a barrel racer you might be surprised at what you can do."

Kari basked in the warmth of his praise. She sat down in the living room and began sorting out the boxes. With the show bill in front of them, they went through and checked the various awards. John pulled out the club's checkbook and they attached the amounts to the first three places for each class.

It was pretty late when they finished arranging all of the awards by classes. Kari went to get them each a cold drink, and John stretched out in the middle of the floor.

He looked wistful as Kari bent over to hand him the Coke. "It's great the way your parents support what you want to do." John laughed. "I think they even approve of your choice."

Kari had to admit, as far as parents went, hers were pretty much all right. She got the impression that John did not feel the same way.

He rolled over on his stomach and studied his Coke can. "It's not that my parents disapprove, so much as they believe I'm setting my sights too high."

Kari had to ask. "Do they know about your scholarship?"

John shook his head. "Not yet." He pushed himself up. "But it should help ease the burden a little bit. Things have been pretty tight since the accident."

Kari had to know more. "Was one of your parents in an accident?"

"My father. A tractor overturned on him. He has been in and out of the hospital ever since. It's been pretty tough on him."

Kari thought it must have been pretty tough on John, too.

He probably had to take on a lot of responsibility. Maybe that was why he seemed more mature than Tim. As far as she knew, Tim had never had any responsibility.

"Was your father a farmer?" she asked.

"Not really," John answered. "He managed Dr. Ackers's farm for him. He was in charge of everyone who worked the farm and he took care of the horses. He was a pretty good trainer, too. Since Dad's accident, they don't work the farm much. It's mostly used for the horses now."

John got up to go. He suddenly looked very tired as he placed the empty soda can in Kari's hand. "I'd better shove off; I have a long day tomorrow. I was hoping we would get a chance to work Poco tonight, but I guess it will have to wait."

Kari walked with him to the back door. What he had told her this evening explained a lot. Now she understood why Dr. Ackers had adopted such a protective attitude towards his protégé and why John worked for the veterinarian at his farm as well as the clinic. She figured Dr. Ackers had had a hand in securing the scholarship as well.

She'd wondered many times in the last couple of weeks where John had acquired his training ability at such an early age. Now she knew—his father had been a trainer.

The only question left unanswered was why his attitude toward her would swing from hot to cold and back again. She wondered if she would ever find out.

The following weekend was the club's horse show. On Thursday, John drove by after work to check on Poco's progress.

As he and Kari started toward the barn, Pam ran out the back door. "Hey, mind if I tag along?"

John looked around. "Not at all. In fact, we might even put you to work."

The three of them entered the barn. Every wall and rafter was covered with plastic flags, balloons, and various other junk, while on a hook hung a brightly colored umbrella. In the middle of this comic array stood Poco, calm and sedate, while all around him balloons bobbed and flags flapped.

"This place looks a little like a circus tent," observed Pam.

"Yes." Kari laughed. "Remind me never to consult him on decorating a room."

John scowled. "Oh, you two are going to gang up on me

today, huh? Wait until I get you in the ring." He looked at
Pam. "Why don't you saddle your pony? I want Poco to work
with another horse in the ring today."

They saddled the two horses and took them to the practice
ring.

"Take them around a couple of laps," John instructed.

Kari could feel his eyes on her as she jogged Poco twice
around the enclosed area. Even though they had worked together
on her horse's problem, it made her nervous to have him watch
her so closely. This was the first time Poco was working without
the running martingale fastened to his saddle and bridle. Kari
prayed that he would continue to set his head correctly.

John stepped to the side of the ring to halt the red horse.
"All right! We're in business." He patted Poco on the neck and
smiled up at Kari. "Looks as though he's going to work okay.
The real test is how he behaves in the show ring, but we won't
know that until Sunday."

John took a step back toward the center of the ring. "Now,
we're going to work this the same way as a class. Pretend I'm
the judge."

"Do we have to?" moaned Kari. She was already so tense
that she was afraid she was going to upset Poco.

"It's so we can pick out any weak spots," said John. He
motioned for Kari to start.

She moved the sorrel from a walk to a jog to a canter at
John's instructions, all the while painfully aware of his watchful
assessment.

John indicated for her to stop and bring Poco to the center
of the ring. Kari did as she was told, stopping him and squaring
him up in the stance of the Western Pleasure horse. She held
her breath, waiting for John's criticism.

"Not bad," he said. "Poco is holding his head beautifully."

Kari breathed a sigh of relief.

"Now for the bad news." He glanced up at Kari. "You're
too stiff in the saddle. You need to relax a little."

How could she relax when she was so afraid of making a
mistake?

John took hold of the stirrup and moved Kari's leg forward.
"The only other thing is adjusting your leg position a little
forward. I noticed you were rocking slightly at the canter."

Kari moved her other leg forward to be in line with the one

John had adjusted. She nudged Poco into a canter and worked him several times around the ring. She felt like shouting for joy when she heard John yell, "That's it. Perfect."

13

IF KARI could have designed a perfect morning, Sunday would have filled the order. The air was fresh and clear after a minor thunderstorm during the night. A hint of a breeze played through the large maples along the edge of the pasture and the sky was a deep blue—the color of John's eyes, Kari thought, raising her face to the early morning sunshine.

The grass was still wet, and Kari's tennis shoes squished as she crossed the backyard from the barn. She paused on the back porch to watch Lynn and Mr. Williams loading Chief. The big horse seemed unusually calm. She watched her friend for several minutes. She hardly ever saw Lynn anymore, and she hadn't really talked to her since the day of Poco's accident. She didn't know if Lynn was intentionally avoiding her or if they were both so busy their paths didn't cross.

"Hurry up," called Mrs. Stewart from the kitchen, "or you won't have time to eat."

When John arrived, they loaded the awards and their equipment into the truck. John opened the back of the walk-in trailer, and Kari loaded Poco. The big red horse hesitated only a moment while he sniffed at the strange horse on the other side of the divider. John tied up his head, and Kari went to climb in the cab. She hopped up into the seat and slid over to allow room for Pam. As usual, her heart began to pound when John climbed into the driver's seat beside her. She was glad the drive to the show grounds was a fairly short one. The closeness to John was doing strange things to her. She tried to concentrate on what he was saying about the day's coming events, but all she could think about was his body just inches from her own. She kept her eyes straight forward, willing her mind to take in the passing scenery.

When they reached the grounds, John stopped the truck by the entry booth. They unloaded the awards before parking the truck and trailer in a shady spot not far from the ring.

Their club advisor was at the hub of the activity shouting directions and getting everyone organized. Some of the parents set up the refreshment stand and soon the smell of Sloppy Joes drifted over the morning breeze. Two of the boys in the club were checking out the PA system by telling rotten jokes over the loudspeaker. Mr. Cooper cut the electric power and sent them to find the obstacles for the trail class. By ten o'clock, the vacant field had become a blur of activity.

Kari returned to the entry booth to set up the display of awards. She cleared the end of a table and carefully lined up the trophies. At the very front and right in the center, she placed the High Point trophy. Running a wire between two of the support posts of the booth, Kari hung the ribbons, each class on a separate coat hanger. They fluttered in the breeze and caught the sun like so many rainbows. Her task completed, Kari returned to the trailer to get Poco ready to show.

"Poco is all ready," announced Pam, running a hand over her sweating forehead as Kari approached.

Kari pulled the saddles from the storage area of the trailer and set them up on end. "Thanks," Kari said. "That really helps."

"Oh, I had some help."

Kari looked around. "By the way, where is John?"

Pam giggled. "John is getting the entry booth organized, but that's not who I was referring to."

Kari shook her head and laughed. "You couldn't possibly mean Steve, now, could you?"

Pam's eyes sparkled and her voice was exuberant. "Oh, Kari, would you believe he asked me to go to the club's hayride and barn dance with him? He actually asked me for a date." Pam danced around in a circle. "My very first date."

The hayride, thought Kari. It was the club's big social event of the summer. They had it every year after the horse show to celebrate a job well done. Kari looked at her sister with envy.

"Do you think Mom and Dad will let me go?" Pam's face was troubled. "I think they would consider it if we went with you. Would you mind?"

Kari wasn't sure she wanted to go this year. In years past, Lynn, Pam, and Kari had gone as a group, along with some of the other girls in the club. But this year it would be different. A couple of the girls were already going with boys, and even her younger sister had a date. Kari examined Pam's animated face. She knew if she didn't go, her sister probably wouldn't be allowed to go with a date.

"Okay," agreed Kari. "I'll drive and play chaperone."

Pam squealed and hugged her. "You're the best sister ever."

Kari laughed and backed away. "Don't get carried away. After all, this may cost you."

Pam made a face. "I already groomed your horse. Don't tell me you're going to force me into slave labor for the next week." She picked up a currycomb and started running it in circular motions over John's little mare. "John said I could show Ginger this afternoon," she said changing the subject. Pam patted the mare lovingly. "She's so pretty."

"And well-trained," added Kari. "You ought to do pretty well with her." She lifted the saddle onto Poco's back and pulled the cinch tight. "You'd better get changed now; your class is one of the first. I'll saddle Ginger for you."

Kari found an open spot along the rail and waited for Pam's class to enter the ring. John came and stood beside her. He folded his arms along the top rail and rested his chin on his forearm. Kari smiled up at him. "Thanks for letting Pam use your little mare."

John turned to look at her. His eyes were shaded by his cowboy hat, but the smile he gave her was dazzling. "Anything for my favorite person's sister."

The words rang in Kari's ears. Was she really his favorite person or was he flirting with her again? Kari was confused and her feelings were in turmoil again. She forced herself to pay attention to the class as Pam rode into the ring. John made comments throughout the performance, pointing out the good and bad points of each rider in the Junior Horsemanship class. Kari was always surprised at his knowledge, but as he continued to instruct her, she began picking up the good points on her own. By the time the class was finished, Kari prided herself on being able to pick the two top riders.

When the class finished, the three of them returned to the trailer. John was leading Ginger, and Pam was proudly carrying her third-place ribbon.

"I've never placed this high before," she said, hanging the ribbon from the rearview mirror of the truck so it wouldn't get crushed.

John smiled. "After you know what the judges are looking

for, you have to keep that in mind. Some people know what to do, but they have trouble doing it."

The afternoon was clear and hot, and the show progressed smoothly. John won a first in his Eighteen-and-older Horsemanship class, Pam picked up a second in Junior Pleasure and even Lynn had won a third-place ribbon.

Kari watched her as she rode up on Chief. They had spoken briefly when Lynn first arrived, but hadn't talked since. Kari missed her friendship. It left an empty space in her life. She wished whatever was wrong between them could be resolved.

Lynn dismounted and looped Chief's reins through the metal ring on the trailer. Her round blue eyes held a sadness Kari had never seen before.

"I've wanted to talk to you," she said. She reached over to stroke Poco's neck, apparently to avoid looking at Kari. "We've been best friends for a long time." Lynn's voice broke and a single tear rolled down her cheek. "I feel so guilty."

Kari touched her arm lightly. "Guilty about what? I don't understand." Kari shook her head in dismay. "You're not talking about Poco's accident, are you?"

Lynn kept her back to Kari. "Yes, Poco . . . and a lot of other things."

When Lynn didn't turn to face her, Kari pulled her hand back from her friend's arm. "But you weren't responsible for what happened to Poco. It was a freak accident." Kari walked around her horse so she could face Lynn. "If anyone is to blame, I am. I should have done something about Poco's head-shyness months ago." She ran her fingers absently up and down the sorrel's muzzle. "But I didn't know what to do."

Lynn raised a tear-stained face. "You don't understand." A pained expression crossed her features. "It's all my fault—everything—I didn't do anything right."

Kari was bewildered. "What are you talking about?"

Their friendship had been strained since before school was out. Lynn's attitude towards her had become increasingly confusing, but nothing as strange as her behavior at that moment.

Lynn let her arms drop to her sides in a hopeless gesture. "The bad trailer, Chief acting up—everything."

Kari studied the ground. What was Lynn going to tell her? She already knew she had lied about working the night she was supposed to put a deposit on the trailer.

Kari continued to stare at the ground. "Chief always acts

up; we both know that." She tried to give Lynn the benefit of the doubt.

"But he didn't have to this time. That's what I'm trying to tell you." Lynn folded her arms and turned her back. Releasing a tired sigh, she swung back around to face Kari. "Dr. Ackers gave me some tranquilizers to give Chief before I tried to load him, but I was afraid to give them to him."

Kari nodded sympathetically. "I can understand that. I would probably have the same problem."

"But they're harmless. I gave him one this morning so we could load him." Lynn squeezed her eyes shut and shook her head. "I don't know why I didn't listen to the vet in the first place. Then the accident would never have happened."

Kari spoke without thinking. "The ramp may still have given way." The moment the words were out, she realized Lynn already felt guilty about the trailer and she was just adding to those feelings. "I'm sorry, I didn't mean . . ."

"No. You're right. The trailer was my responsibility that time, and I blew it. I forgot all about going down to the rental place and putting a deposit on a good trailer."

Kari pressed for the truth. "You forgot? I thought you were working and didn't have time."

Lynn's face wore the look of a child caught with her hand in the cookie jar. She walked over to the trailer and sank against the wheel well. "Well, I guess you might as well know all of it." Lynn's voice held a sound of defeat. "I didn't want to tell you the part about Tim."

"Tim!" Kari nearly shouted the name. "What's he got to do with this?" Images of the scene in the driveway the day Poco was injured flowed through her memory. That image was followed by others—the day Tim came to the horse show, the party where he was so concerned about Lynn being bored, and her friend's constant questions about how she and Tim were getting along. Kari felt she was getting a pretty clear picture of what Lynn was about to tell her, and she wasn't sure she wanted to hear. She hoped she was wrong.

"Kari, I don't want to hurt you," Lynn began. "He is your boyfriend—"

"If you're trying to tell me you're dating Tim, I—"

"No," Lynn interrupted. "I never went out with him even though he asked. He still asks me, but I keep turning him down."

"But he's not my boyfriend," Kari argued. "Not anymore. Not since the night of the party. Was he asking you out before then?"

"What?" Lynn almost choked. "But I've seen his car at your house a couple of times since then, and I see him drive by all the time. I thought he was going to see you."

Kari sank down on the wheel well next to Lynn. "He did come by a couple of times, but all he did was make trouble, so I told him to get lost. I guess he neglected to tell you that."

"He sort of forgot to mention that," Lynn said in disgust. "He's an even bigger rat than I thought. He just keeps telling me that you would never find out if I went out with him."

Lynn scowled. "In answer to your other question . . ." She hesitated and Kari begged her to continue. "Yes, he did ask me out while he was still supposedly going with you. The first time was at the show when Poco fell." She looked sideways at Kari. "That's why I kept asking all those dumb questions. I had to know where you stood with Tim, whether you were going to get hurt or not." Lynn sighed deeply. "I was hoping you would get interested in someone else, someone a little more worthy."

"You mean you're not interested in him?"

Lynn shook her head. "No way. I have to admit I was very attracted to him at first, even though I didn't like the way he treated you. It seemed like he was everything I wanted—good-looking, popular, a member at the club, and then I realized he had nothing meaningful to offer. He only uses people."

"Uses people?" Kari was puzzled. She wasn't sure how she had been used.

"Like with you," Lynn answered. "I think he liked you, at least as well as he could like anyone, but how many times did he come over to see you, and end up having your father help him with his math homework?"

"But my father didn't mind."

"That's not the point," insisted Lynn. "Do you know where he was the last couple of weeks when you two weren't getting along? When he didn't meet you for lunch?" Lynn paused dramatically. "Being tutored in Trig, that's where. When your father wasn't accessible, he had to find someone else. I'm sure that's the only reason he was seeing Diane, so she could tutor him during lunch."

"Diane?" Kari repeated, making the connection. "You mean

Diane Palmer, the new senior?" So the rumors she had heard at the end of school were true.

Lynn stood up and walked a few steps away from the trailer. "And do you know why he was chasing me?" Lynn's voice rose in pitch as her anger increased. "Because my dad was managing the swimming pool. Do you know how many times he tried to get me to ask my dad for special privileges and after-hours parties? That's when I began to see the truth."

Lynn balled her fists and stomped her foot. "The nerve of that jerk. He called the night I was supposed to reserve the trailer. When I said I wouldn't go out with him, he said he was dropping by to see me anyway." Lynn looked helplessly at Kari. "I didn't know what to do. I didn't want you to see his car at my house and think I was going out with him behind your back. I took off and went shopping so I wouldn't be there. That's why I forgot all about the trailer."

Kari stared at the ground. "What a big dope I was. What a complete idiot."

Lynn walked back to the trailer and stopped in front of Kari. "That's not true. You always look for the good in someone and trust people. But a creep like Tim doesn't deserve that kind of trust." She shuffled her feet uncomfortably. "I'm sorry I made a mess of things. I guess I should have told you the truth right from the beginning."

Kari smiled sadly. "It wasn't your fault."

"Then we can be friends again?" Lynn attempted a smile.

"We never stopped being friends," Kari said. She stood up and wrinkled her nose at Lynn. "Looks like it's back to just the two of us."

"Not exactly," giggled Lynn. She stepped back and Kari noticed a pinkish tinge to her cheeks. "Do you remember the guy I was with at the party?"

Kari nodded. "Doug."

"I think he's the greatest guy I ever met. We've only been out a couple of times, but I think I'm in love." Lynn smiled happily. "Really in love." Her face was glowing as she looked at Kari. "I invited him on the club's hayride next weekend, and he said he'd come."

"I'm really glad for you." Then a little sadly she added, "It looks like I'm the only one without a date for next weekend."

"Don't be so sure," teased Lynn. "I think there's someone who might ask you. He sure hangs around you enough."

"You mean John?" Kari shook her head. "We work together. We've become good friends, that's all."

"No, it's more than that," argued Lynn. "I saw the way he looked at you the very first night you met. No one else even had a chance of catching his attention. For what my opinion is worth, I think he's terrific." Lynn hugged her quickly and said, "I'd better let you get to your class. And don't forget, hint to John about the hayride."

Kari stepped into the saddle. She smiled down at Lynn as she turned Poco toward the make-up ring.

A crazy excitement ran through her. Could John really be interested? Lynn seemed to think so. Kari dared to hope. If Lynn was right, then why hadn't he told her so?

Entering the ring, Kari scanned the rail for John. He was standing just past the entrance and waved to catch her attention. Kari smiled and glanced sideways as she passed him on the rail.

"Relax," he said under his breath. "You're too stiff."

Relax, thought Kari, if only she could. She was giddy with happiness and had to concentrate on the commands from the loudspeaker. After all the time she and John had spent getting ready for this show, she didn't want to blow it.

Kari forced her full attention to the task at hand. She worked Poco through his paces and was only slightly aware of John's penetrating gaze from the side of the ring. Poco had never worked better. He set his head without so much as a toss and worked all his gaits with precision and accuracy. When the ringmaster called the class to the center of the ring, Kari knew she had done well. She also knew John was watching her and returned his look triumphantly.

The loudspeaker crackled to life. Kari held her breath. "The winner of Senior Horsemanship is number..."

Kari couldn't believe her ears. It was her number! For one long second she sat stunned.

"Move, beautiful," John yelled from the rail.

Kari walked Poco forward. Her fingers were shaking as she reached down for the golden statue. It felt cold and smooth as she wrapped her fingers around its graceful curves. Her surroundings became a blur, and Kari was only aware of the shining blue of the first-place ribbon as it was placed in her hand with the trophy.

She trotted Poco from the ring. Tears ran down her cheeks

as she found John's face in the crowd. His strong hands circled her waist and lifted her from the saddle. He swung her around several times, hugging her close. Kari threw her arms around his neck and hugged him back. Then, aware they were standing in a crowd, she dropped her arms and stepped back. John looked into her eyes, and what Kari read in their blue depths made her heart sing.

They walked hand in hand to the trailer. She set the trophy on the flat wheel well and stepped back to admire its metallic beauty.

John came up behind her and she could feel his breath as it fanned her neck. The sensation sent little shivers of pleasure down her spine.

"I'm so proud of you," he said close to her ear. He placed his hands on her shoulders and turned her around to face him. "The way you handled the awards for the show, and then what you've done with Poco. I knew you could do it."

Kari's eyes shone. "We did it—together—the two of us."

John's gaze swept over her face lovingly. "We make a pretty unbeatable team."

"Are we a team, John?"

A guarded look came over his face. "I'd like to be. I'd like to be more than that, but I don't think your fancy boyfriend would approve."

"My fancy boyfriend? Oh, you mean Tim. He's not my boyfriend."

"You aren't seeing him anymore?"

Kari shook her head. "Not since that night we worked late in the lab and I had to leave to go to the party."

"But I saw him at your house after that."

"I know," Kari answered. "He was just there to make trouble." Kari had come to realize in the last few weeks that Tim couldn't stand to lose—at anything. He had viewed her breaking up with him as losing. He wasn't about to accept that without causing some trouble.

She looked into the blue depths of John's eyes, and her troubles with Tim were forgotten. "I couldn't be interested in anyone else after I met you."

The guarded look fell away and a faint light twinkled in his beautiful eyes. "I felt the same way from the first night I met you, but I kept seeing you with that guy in the expensive sports car."

"He did have a way of showing up at the wrong time."

John smiled sheepishly. "Like every time I worked up enough courage to ask you out."

Kari looked at him shyly from under lowered lashes. "Well, he's not here now."

John reached out and caught her hands in his. He pulled her close so his face was only a few inches from hers. "Kari— would you go to the club's hayride and dance with me next week?"

Kari couldn't believe her ears. She was actually going on a date with John, to be snuggled next to him in the hay wagon and to be held close in his arms at the barn dance.

She raised her face to his and tears of joy filled her green eyes. She nodded mutely. John wrapped her gently in his arms. He bent his dark head and lightly touched his lips to hers. Pulling back, he looked at her face intently. She knew all her love for him was written there. She reached up and wrapped her arms around his neck.

"There's something I've been wanting to tell you," he said, his voice husky. It was a soft whisper on his lips as he lowered his head to kiss her again. "I love you, Kari."

Now that you're reading the best in teen romance, why not make that *Caprice* feeling part of your own special look? Four great gifts to accent that "unique something" in you are all yours when you collect the proof-of-purchase from the back of any current *Caprice* romance!

Each proof-of-purchase is worth 3 Heart Points toward these items available <u>only</u> from *Caprice*. And what better way to make them yours than by reading the romances every teen is talking about! Start collecting today!

Proof-of-purchase is worth 3 Heart Points toward one of four exciting premiums bearing the distinctive *Caprice* logo

CAPRICE PREMIUMS
Berkley Publishing Group, Inc./Dept. LB
200 Madison Avenue, New York, NY 10016

PROOF OF
PURCHASE
—3—
HEART POINTS
DETAILS INSIDE

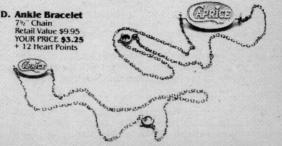